Joseph Mayo

Woodbourne

A novel of the Revolutionary period in Virginia and Maryland. Part 1

Joseph Mayo

Woodbourne
A novel of the Revolutionary period in Virginia and Maryland. Part 1

ISBN/EAN: 9783337000530

Printed in Europe, USA, Canada, Australia, Japan

Cover: Foto ©Andreas Hilbeck / pixelio.de

More available books at **www.hansebooks.com**

WOODBOURNE:

A Novel of the Revolutionary Period in Virginia
and Maryland.

IN TWO PARTS.

BY COLONEL JOSEPH MAYO.

PART I.

BALTIMORE:
PUBLISHED BY JOHN B. PIET & CO.,
174 West Baltimore Street.
1881.

DEDICATION.

TO COLONEL ROBERT M. MAYO
(of Auburn, in the County of Westmoreland, Virginia),
as a Slight Token of the Author's Gratitude for
his numberless acts of more than Brotherly
Kindness, this Volume is Affectionately Inscribed.

PREFACE.

THE principal events recorded in these pages relate to the most interesting epoch of American history. The scene is chiefly confined to a little spot of that "Land within the Capes," which its first explorer has described as bearing the prerogative over the most pleasant places known. In our unambitious narrative, which is concerned with the fortunes of two or three families, we profess to deal with subjects of general public interest only as they may serve to elucidate the main design. We do not propose to write a society novel, nor yet a pure romance, nor to try and bedizen a prosy array of unimportant events in the trumpery garb of sentimental fancy. Much less shall we undertake to draw an elaborate picture of the every-day manners and customs of the ancient proverbial cavaliers of Virginia—cavaliers still in spite of the disgust which some people affect to have for the name. Yet in giving to the American public our "poor account of rich doings," we deem it eminently proper to devote a short space to the task of correcting some of the erroneous impressions of our fatherland and its inhabitants which have gone abroad unchallenged over the face of the earth. First and foremost, then, let it be distinctly affirmed that the Vir-

ginians of that day were no more Mr. Thackaray's
"Virginians" than is the country in which they dwelt
the same which is prefigured in the chart of his fruitful
imagination. True, their landed possessions were in
several instances as large as many a petty European
principality; and the owners of such vast domains were,
doubtless, entitled to as great consideration as any beg-
garly landgrave or boorish count palatine, yet it is a
figment of prurient fancy to suppose that these manorial
nabobs all lived in solitary habitations twenty miles apart
each from his neighbor, and surrounded by savage wilds
where, as the nursery rhymer says,

> "Naked men in forests prowled,
> And bears and panthers roamed and howled."

And whatever may have been their capacity for getting
over the ground, they surely were not equal to the task
of performing impossible journeys over impassible roads
in preposterous yellow vehicles, "carrying six insides."
In all seriousness, if the chief merit of fiction consists,
as Macauley has remarked, in its resemblance to a model
with which we are already familiar or to which we can
constantly refer, in the name of the fairy muse what
shall be said of the incongruous brood of extravagan-
cies which one sees in the Virginia booth of Mr. Thackaray's teeming bazaar? When Colonel Henry Esmond—
the only fine, real gentleman who figures in his own
memoirs—sought at once refuge from villainous company
and balm and solace from gout and *ennui* amid the
charming solitude of his plantation in Virginia, it is certain that he found the moral atmosphere of his new

abode to be a vast improvement on the mephitic impurities of the *grotto-del-carne*, from which he had escaped in a half-asphyxiated condition. Here, at least, he was rid of the beastly Yahoos of Vanity Fair. Here the unsophisticated country people called things by their given names. My Lord Mohun, the grand sachem of the civilized Mohocks, was rated as a consummate ruffian and knave, and the fairest of the frail nymphs of St. Germain's and Soho square was a very Hecate of moral deformity because of the shame,

> "Which, like a canker in the fragrant rose,
> Did spot the beauty of her budding name."

The votaries of fashion, the roues of the salon and boudoir, the maccaronis of the club-house and the gambling den, the starveling villipenders of Grub street, the swarms of seedy political pimps, panders and prostitutes, were in their eyes the same disgusting caricatures of humanity, whether paraded in Steele and Addison's polished periods, or pilloried by Pope and Swift in "Images from the dunghill and lazar house." These were the early and late associates and boon-companions of this courtly chronicler of scandalous small beer, who would make us believe that half the women in England of that day would have been most profitably employed in beating hemp in Bridewell to make "cravats" for three-fourths of the men. The world he has described is that in which the dramatic fancy of Congreve and Wycherly revelled with delight, where "the women were like profligate, impudent and unfeeling men, and where the men were too bad for any place but Pandemonium and Norfolk Island." What, after all, is this tiresome

old male gossip, but one of those "coxcomb birds, so
talkative and grave," who from his cage pelts the passers-
by with ribald words and scurvy jests?

"Though many a passenger he rightly call,
We hold him no philosopher-at all."

With like indignant emphasis do we repudiate the exag-
gerated portraits of our good ancestors which grace the
galleries of certain native artists, who appear to labor
under the strange delusion that the subjects of their
delineations spent the best part of their lives in stalking
around the circle of stiltish, purse-proud arrogance, and
swaggering in a "high-kilted" Babylonish dialect, which
out-gasconaded Gascony. It is farthest from the truth,
moreover, to suppose that the typical Virginian cavalier
found his only pleasures in fox-hunting and cock-fighting;
carousing in tap-rooms, and wrangling over cards and
dice, betting at races, and whispering vapid sentiment
in the ear of simpering beauty. On the contrary, he
was as exquisitely alive and keenly sensitive as any
"mortal mixture of earth's mold' to those lofty impressions and delicate touches of feeling and passion which
elevate the soul, expand the intellect, enliven the fancy,
kindle in the heart the generous flame of sympathy and
love, and strew with flowers the thorny paths of life.
And in the hour of severest trial, when Red Battle's
stern alarum rung out over hill and dale, he approved
himself a manly, robust, bold and independent freeman,
who bared his bosom to the howling storm and recked
not of danger and sacrifice in his country's cause. Of
Toryism, as the term was applied during the Revolu-

tionary era, there was little or nothing in this part of the Old Dominion. All classes and conditions of the people were more nearly united in thought, feeling and purpose than had been the case in any civil disturbance previously recorded in English history. Still, there were not a few among the wealthy and most influential planters who dreaded to cut loose all of a sudden from the ancient moorings and set out on a voyage of exploration "in thick weather on an unknown sea." They were not able by a single effort to break the ties, "light as air and strong as links of iron," which bound them to the time-honored institutions, hoary traditions, and immemorial usages of their fathers. They cherished a fond veneration of the aristocratic and monarchical features of the constitution, for the canons of property and laws of descent, for the wholesome restrictions upon the elective franchise and the right to hold office, and in regarding the freedom and safety of the subject as the origin and cause of all laws; they nevertheless believed that the principles to which they were so ardently attached afforded the only secure bulwarks and muniments of right and justice. They read, with avidity, the letters of Junius, and applauded' the burning utterances of Burke and Chatham; but they were not prepared to receive, without debate, the precepts of the sage of Gunston, nor to hear without trepidation the inspired voice of the SEER, "whose thunder shook the Philip of the Seas." As hostilities advanced, their minds were gradually changed, and they became in the end zealous supporters of the cause of American freedom. To the influence of this class—wise, prudent, high-minded and determined

men—was mainly due the auspicious result that, in the
formation of the Republic, the spirit of innovation was
restrained within the confines of just and rational re-
form.

But our "prolegomenon" is growing into a tedious historical dissertation. Not to make too sudden a "pull-up,"
we take occasion to repeat that in the following pages
we have striven to produce a popular work of fiction
which should be catholic in spirit, national in tone, free
from sectional and sectarian bias and prejudice, and con-
taining not a word or thought, hint or allusion, of ques-
tionable propriety. As such it is kindly commended to
the appreciative consideration of the American people.

CONTENTS.

PART I.

WOODBOURNE.

PART I.

CHAPTER I.

ONE of her own native bards has sung in mournful numbers the miseries of "hapless Caledonia," doomed to reap the bitterest fruits of the last bloody harvest of internecine strife which ripened in gory ghastliness on the soil of Britain. It is no horrid dream of phrenzied imagination, the tragic picture we are gazing upon; but the frightful reality of calamitous woe, fell-born progeny of the grisly demon of civil discord and fratricidal rage.

Scotland, indeed, was made to feel its keenest pangs; but the terrible scourge did not confine its ravages to her ill-fated borders. It carried desolation and mourning to many a happy English home, and everywhere inflicted great gaping wounds on the bosom of society, which, for long years to come, broke out and bled afresh at the whisper of some name of hateful memory and portentous sound.

Have they been wholly healed by the great physician, Time? For the sake of all that humanity holds dear, let us so hope and believe. Who so basely vile and malevolent as would wish to see again the fiery signal of insurrection cast its baleful gleam across that fair horizon, whence the genius of Christian civilization from its island throne instructs the nations in the victorious arts of Peace.

It is necessary, for the elucidation of these pages, for us to take a flying trip across the ocean. We are now in the midst of the beautiful region which has been appropriately styled the Arcadia of Scotland. The scene is a small villa near the banks of Leven Water; and time, an evening in the leafy month of June, in the year 1753. It has been raining—a passing thunder shower. The sun has just come forth from his vapory bath, and every bush and brake is hailing his reappearance with warbling pæans of surpassing melody. The fleecy clouds, all radiant with prismatic glories, are slowly trooping towards the east, and the last faint peal of heaven's artillery reverberates far down the vale. On every twig and blade of grass the pearly raindrops are sparkling bright; the air is laden with the rich perfume of blossoming flowers; on the mountains the heather blooms with a deeper purple, and the dimpling wavelets of the limpid stream dance merrily in the shimmering sunlight.

Two ladies are seated at an open window which commands a delightful prospect, embracing the most bewitching features of the extensive landscape. One is old; yet the frosts of age have not chilled her heart, which speaks in the look of tender affection and solicitude with which she is regarding her companion. The latter lady is in the early prime and loveliness of charming womanhood. Her face wears an expression of sadness, which appears to be foreign to her natural disposition. She is resting her chin on one hand; in the other is an open letter, and her large, grey eyes, moist with springing tears, are gazing absently at the distant cloud-pavilioned crag towards which the sun is rapidly declining. To a long and earnest conversation, which was not without painful interest to the young lady, there had ensued a silence of some moments' duration. It was broken by the elder lady.

"All happens for the best, my child," she said, meeting an outburst of disappointment with the golden commonplace of old age's proverbial philosophy. "I was convinced from the first that the effort would prove fruitless; yet I did not try to dissuade you from making it, because I knew you would not be satisfied until you had done everything in your power to discover what was your brother's fate; now your mind is at ease on that account. You cannot justly reproach yourself with having left undone anything which sisterly affection and duty commanded you to do, and you will soon forget this heavy affliction in your new home, amid untried scenes and cares."

"It is impossible for me ever to forget it, dear aunt," replied the other lady; "but with God's help it shall not be the means of bringing a single pang of unhappiness to others. True, as you say, there is an end of my long cherished hope;—this letter assures me of it; but I must beg you to repeat the story over again as Uncle Leslie heard it from the dying lips of our cousin, Duncan Campbell; I fain would impress every syllable of it on my memory in indellible characters. It may seem to be a weak and frivolous fancy to you, and I am certainly unable to explain it; yet only a witness from the grave can dispel the strange tormenting presentiment I have that my brother escaped alive from that bloody field."

"If such was the incredulous state of your mind, Ellen, after having once heard Duncan's clear story," said her aunt, gravely, "I do not see what good can come of worrying yourself with trying to remember it. However, you know best. Perhaps it may in time dispel the wicked illusion which harasses you with constant anxiety, and to gratify you, I will relate the story once more as your uncle told it to me. Poor Duncan! he was another dear victim of that sinful rebellion. Oh, those wretched times! how it makes me shudder to revive the recollection of them. I must be brief, my dear, for it is not pleasant to dwell on this painful subject. Duncan, as you are aware, was serving on the staff of his kinsman, the Duke of Argyle. He had learned that your brother, whom he loved dearly, had, in a freak of madness, left Oxford and enlisted with the Chevalier's party at Derby; and all the time the battle was going on at Culloden he was looking everywhere for the miserable boy to take him prisoner, believing that with Argyle's influence there would be no difficulty in getting a pardon for him. It was not until the battle was over, and the poor misguided rebels were flying in every direction, that he came upon the object of his search. A little band of the bravest of Charles Edwards' followers, seeing the day was lost, had made a gallant stand in order to enable their leader to make good his escape; with them was your brother. His hat was gone, and a stream of blood was pouring from a ghastly wound on his head, and he fought as one fights who courts death on the field of battle. Brave boy, alas! alas! that he should have been reserved for such a fate." Aunt Leslie paused to wipe the gathering moisture from her eyes, while her niece, with a convulsive sob, buried her face in her hands, as seeking to shut out the horrible scene. "Duncan," resumed the old lady, "as soon as he saw his cousin, pressed eagerly towards him through the thickest of the fray. Presently, he beheld him suddenly reel in his saddle and fall to the ground; at the same instant he himself was struck in the breast by the fatal bullet and borne away lifeless, as was thought, from the field. When he returned to consciousness he found himself lying upon a pallet of straw in a farm house close to the battle-ground, and in the first words that he spoke he begged them to go and search for your brother, describing as well as he could the spot where he had seen him fall. His entreaties were promptly obeyed. A diligent search was made for the body; it was not found. Still Duncan was not satisfied. Next day, at his request, a squad of men were detailed by the Duke's order to prosecute the unavailing search, and when the officer in charge of them, who was selected by Duncan himself,

1*

reported another failure, the poor lad at last despaired of ever finding his unfortunate kinsman's remains. His own wound was mortal; he was taken home, where he lived only a short month more. In his dying hour his mind wandered back to the terrible battlefield, and Henry's name was the last word his lips were heard to speak. And now, Ellen, since all efforts to find your brother have been in vain, we are forced to conclude, after listening to this circumstantial narration, that he was numbered among the dead on that woful day at Culloden Muir. Tell me, my love, what did John say when he heard your tragical story?"

A sudden glow, rivalling the tints of the sky she had been looking upon, mantled the beautiful face of the young lady, and her tearful eye shone with a brightness which was akin to rapture.

"Oh, aunt!" she exclaimed, "I imagined before that I loved and respected him with my whole heart, but I never dreamed of falling at his feet and worshipping him until that moment. When I saw him looking at me with such an expression of love and sympathy and tender compassion, no words can portray. I could not help crying as though my heart was breaking, while all the time it was running over with joy and gratitude. It was very weak and foolish, but he knew the cause— so noble and good, so gentle and considerate. Then we quietly talked it all over again, and agreed that it was best for the happiness of others that it should remain forever a sealed chapter in the book of our wedded lives."

"I am truly rejoiced to hear you speak of John

in that way, my dear child," replied Mrs. Leslie; "he was always a great favorite with me from a boy. You were rather slow to consult me, but he is the man of all others I would have picked out for your husband. Yet I am sadly loth to give you up, for I know I shall never see you again in this world, you will be so far away. How many miles did John say it was to Virginia?"

"He said thousands, aunt, I do not remember how many; but I feel as though I were really going to live in a world which had nothing in common with this. It grieves me sorely to think of having to part with you, my dearest aunt—you, who are the sole remaining tie which binds me to my native land. You must not then believe I am cold and unfeeling because I long to be quickly transported to those scenes I have never yet beheld, where lies my future home, together with all my hopes of peace and happiness on this earth. My mind is so constantly employed with contemplating the new career which opens before me, that I feel inspired with energies and aspirations and desires of which I have hitherto been unconscious. It is good to know that I was not made to mope and pine in indolent apathy and corroding sorrow. There is the germ of real, earnest, strong and courageous stuff in my nature—my birthright and only inheritance, which, when transplanted to a more generous soil, and fostered with loving care, will one day burst into the full flower of domestic usefulness. Hence, it is natural that I should hail with exceeding joy the approach of the time appointed for me to assume the dignity and responsibility of wifehood, and strive to become as one whose 'husband is known in the gates where he sitteth among the rulers of the land.' For all that, dearest aunt, my heart is none the less warm for you and yours, and whatever *he* may say, I am sure there is no place in America can compare in beauty with this lovely spot."

As she spoke a bird flew down from a neighboring tree, and alighting on a spray of woodbine close by the window, carolled forth a single note of enchanting sweetness. In a moment it was gone. It had come to say good-bye to the pretty lady, and to give her that little gem of song for a keepsake.

"Nor any music like the song of the mavis, my dear," said Aunt Leslie. "Do you believe John's wonderful tales of the mocking birds in Virginia? But of course you do, and all he says about the beautiful flowers growing wild in the woods. Speaking of them, the woods, you must promise me, Ellen, not to venture to go into them unless John goes with you. It was only the other day that I heard our neighbor Smollett telling of a little girl, the daughter of a friend who was living in Virginia somewhere or Jamaica, I am not certain which, but it is all one, who had gone out to hunt for flowers in the forest, and—"

"Was murdered and scalped by the hideous savages!" cried the young lady in a voice of affected horror.

"Not so terrible as that."

"Bitten by one of those frightful rattlesnakes!"

"Not so, either; don't interrupt me, child. As I was saying, the girl was lost in the woods,

and when they found her, after looking ever so
many hours, she was fast asleep under a huge tree,
and her clothes were literally torn to tatters."

The effect of this fearful climacteric showed that
the young lady was not wanting in a keen perception of the ludicrous.

"Why, aunt," she exclaimed, with a ringing laugh,
which chased away the shadow from her pensive
brow, "I was on the tenter-hooks for some awful
catastrophe, and lo! and behold, it is only a story
of one poor babe in the woods with the dear little redbreasts left out. Do not be uneasy on my
account; the flowers may 'a' wede away' in their
native wilds for me; it is the thought of crossing
the great ocean which really alarms my fancy, and
if I get safely through the 'vexed Bermoothes,'
there is no danger of my being lost in the jun-
gles of Virginia. But, oh! aunt, just behold the
sunset; could anything be more magnificent? I
shall carry that away with me among my heart's
treasures, and," she inaudibly added, "the recollection of the dear, sweet face which is turning to
look at it, will abide with me as a joy forever-
more."

Aunt Leslie was touched.

"It is indeed a beautiful sight, my dearest child,"
she fervently responded. "I earnestly pray it may
prove to be the emblem of the evening of a long
and happy life to you."

Again the ready tears gathered in Ellen's lovely
eyes. She hastily rose, and throwing her arms about
her aunt's neck, kissed her affectionately; then she
knelt reverently at her side. Mrs. Leslie softly

drew the sweet suppliant's head towards her until it rested on her bosom, and raising her eyes to heaven, besought its guidance and protection for the lonely orphan who was about to tempt the perils of the deep, to find among strangers, in a strange land, the haven of rest and happiness she had looked for in vain in a country where every object she beheld was tinged with the dark hue of a sorrowful remembrance.

They had remained for a short while in this prayerful attitude, when the sound of carriage wheels was heard approaching the house.

"The gentlemen have returned, Ellen," said Mrs. Leslie, "and soon the friends who are coming to take leave of you will be here. It is time you were dressing for the parlor. There, dry your eyes, and keep the rest of your tears for the hour of parting. John will expect you to wear your warmest smiles to-night, as to-morrow is your wedding-day."

The young lady calmed her agitated feelings as promptly as she could, and proceeded to comply with her aunt's injunction. But before leaving the room, she turned once more to the window, and her glance lingered in a last fond farewell on the beloved images of her girlhood's home. The next morning John Graeme and Ellen Campbell were married, and ere another sun had set they are miles away on their journey to Glasgow, where the ship was waiting which was destined to bear them safely to their pleasant home in the Old Dominion.

Twenty years or more have come and gone. The good Aunt Leslie has been gathered to her fathers these many days; but her prayers have been an-

swered. The junior partner of the famous mercantile house of Ballantine & Graeme has prospered
amazingly, and Ellen has found a home which fills
the measure of anticipated happiness to the very
brim. They call their house Bonhill, in honor of
Mr. Graeme's old friend and school fellow, the
author of *Peregrine Pickle* and the *Ode to Leven
Water*. It is a lovely place, and whilst we do its
sweet mistress the justice to state that she does
not fail on occasion to speak in becoming terms
of admiration of the Arcadian delights, the bonny
burnsides, the flowery braes and fragrant spreading
shaws she left behind her in the Land o' Cakes,
she assuredly appreciates none the less the glowing
charms of this favored clime. She readily admits
that the gorgeous splendors of the autumnal even-
tide in Virginia are enchanting beyond anything
her imagination had foretold, and that the mock-
ing-bird is a very marvel of feathered symphony.
As for the wild flowers, she argues that they flour-
ish most bonnily in their native parterres, among
the rich meadows, the thorny brakes and bosky
hill-slopes; but she prefers to have a garden of
her own,—

And the jessamine sweet, and the sweet tuberose,
The sweetest flower for scent that blows,
And all rare blossoms from every clime
Grow in that garden in perfect prime.

But there are no dusky mountains bristling with
furze and gorse; no crystal river warbling over its
pebbly bed, only the wooded hills and chalky cliffs
of Stratford, and the placid blue waters of the
noble Potomac mirroring the bluer sky. And instead

ot the nut-brown lassie trilling her simple love-
song over the pail, we can hear, if we like, Aunt
Dinah's doleful baritone drowsily crooning some
eldritch catch, as she lazily plies her evening care
of milking the cows. The last comparison, however, is entirely gratuitous, not to say impertinent.
Mrs. Graeme was happily possessed of a rare talent
for music, and had diligently improved the gift, and
the barbarous ditty of milkmaid, brown or black,
was harsh discord to her sensitive ear.

Taken all in all, the lot of Ellen Graeme had
been such as does not fall to many in this vale
of tears, even when we debit the account of happiness with the sorrows and privations of her child-
hood's years. From the moment she set foot on
the threshold of her new home until now, she had
known but one great affliction, in the death of her
oldest child,—a bright little blossom of three years
plucked from its parent stem to deck the heavenly
bowers; and she lived to see the son and daughter,
with whom she was afterwards blest, grow up under
her watchful eye, and become all that a mother's
heart could desire. Her cup of rejoicing was then
full, crowned, overflowing. Nobly had she earned the
sweet reward of woman's highest earthly ambition—
' her children arise up and call her blessed; her
husband also, and he praiseth her." And John
Graeme's praise was no holiday compliment; it was
the constant, free, unstinted offering of tenderest
love and unfailing sympathy. While he did his
duty to his neighbor as a God-fearing man should
do, and was in the truest sense a father to his
children, to his wife he gave the unmeasured devotion of his loyal, manly heart.

CHAPTER II.

ON a bright evening in the early part of the month of November, 1775, a gentleman on horseback, approaching at a canter the brow of the gently sloping declivity which overlooks N——— Ferry, drew rein so suddenly that he seemed to have been riveted to the spot by the wand of enchantment.

Now we protest, most ungentle of critics, there is nothing in this simple prologue to provoke that derisive ejaculation. Go on with the story, and you will presently discover that our cavalier is quite another sort of person from the hackneyed creature you are thinking of. That far from being one of those fantastic images with which the genius of romance has peopled its realm of shadows, yonder solitary horseman is fully endued with the properties of mortal flesh and blood, however much he may be destined to excel the vulgar herd of human kind. Erect and motionless as a statue, he could not have assumed a better attitude were he conscious of having his picture taken by the cleverest of modern photographers. The subject is worthy the pencil of Apelles; but in the absence of the divine artist, we will try our profane hand at a rough and ready sketch.

2

First of all, it is evident that our traveler is decidedly youthful, as his cheek, ruddy-brown from exposure to sun and breeze, is smooth and dimpled as a damsel in her teens, and his chin is innocent of even the rudiments of a beard. At a venture, one might say he was a little the rise of twenty years old. He is a trifle larger than what would be thought the middle size at his age; his form is at once lithe, graceful and compact, and he is withal strikingly fair and comely in every feature and lineament, gesture and glance. For his dress, he is neatly habited in a fashionable drab-colored riding suit, tipped off with plain double gilt buttons, and in lieu of boots his nether limbs are enveloped in a pair of yellow buckskin leggings, which reach nighly to his hips. Like proof of unostentatious refinement is observed in the hat he has on, which is entirely divested of the tawdry embellishments so profusely worn by the young fops of the day. The accoutrements of his horse, a superb bay gelding, meet in all respects for so gallant a rider, are of simple and substantial English workmanship, without ornament of any kind. His pose is the perfection of ideal elegance and ease, betraying in every respect, from the grasp of the nervous hand on the tightened rein, to the light, airy touch of the foot on the polished stirrup, a very prince of the manége whose throne is the saddle. Gathered in a roll, and strapped behind the saddle, is a blue cloth surtout, and thus scantily equipped it is easily inferred that our cavalier is not going a very long journey. Leisure enough, too, he seems to have for indulging the poetical

sensations awakened by the glorious panorama which
has broken upon him like a vision of fairy land.
And surely a lovelier, softer, and more gorgeous landscape never inspired the exquisite soul of Italian
art. On this particular occasion, two rare circumstances conspired to give additional charm to the
scene. The evening was as calm as an infant's
sleep, so that the numberless sounds of rustic music
floated, mellowed and sweetly modulated, on the
downy bosom of the atmosphere. Then the season
had been unusually mild, and the fields and forests had not yet surrendered their rich treasures to
the ravages of "chill November's surly blast";
but bedecked in all the splendor of their many
hued liveries, they displayed the ecstatic harmony
of colors which is the unreached paradise of the
painter's despair. Here and there on the summit of
a gentle eminence the gable, roof or other portion
of a dwelling house peered forth from a bowery
of embosoming groves, and across the open fields
an occasional herd of kine soberly wended their
way to the evening fold. Away in the distance
the majestic "river of swans," its broad face glowing with delight, was enjoying with supreme satisfaction the interval of unwonted repose, and at
your feet the modest little N———, pursuing its
gently winding way round headland and cliff,
appeared like a chain of silvery lakes, whose bright
mirrors gave back with enhanced glory the ravish-
ing loveliness they imbibed. Over all this scene
of varied beauty the slowly sinking sun of an
Indian summer spread its indescribable sheen, and
earth and sky vied with each other to produce

such a masterpiece of Nature's handiwork as would
have kindled adoration in the heart of the coldest
skeptic.

Not many moments was our susceptible cavalier
permitted to remain in rapt contemplation of this
beautiful picture, for now his ear has caught a
familiar sound, that, rising gradually above the
drowsy hum and gathering volume as it approached,
burst all at once so clear and resonant on the
still air as to send the blood rushing through his
veins in a torrent of wild exhiliration. Partaking
the same enthusiasm, the noble courser gave a
great bound forward, and before rider could recover
his seat and bring the full force of the curb to
bear, was speeding away in the direction of the
inspiring sound.

Moralists may homilize to their hearts' content,
but there is no enjoyment so intense and tumul-
tuos to man and horse as the intoxicating revelry
of the chase. Checking his impatient steed, and
galloping back to his post of observation, the
young gentleman reached it just in time to see a
pack of hounds emerge from the cover of the
forest into a large field a short distance beyond the
river. In a twinkling they have crossed it, and
are again lost to view in the pine thickets which
adorn the river's edge with an emerald fringe.
Straight after them, trailing one behind another,
comes a party of fifteen or twenty huntsmen. As
they cross the plain, most of those in rear come
up on a line with the one in front and some pass
him, so that it is now become a headlong race for
the prize which woodland heroes so ardently covet.

Many a ditch, both broad and deep, traverses the
field, but these are easily cleared at a flying leap
by the whole chasing troop. A more serious obstacle
interposes in the shape of an ugly worm-fence,
high and bristling with jagged stakes and uncouth
riders. At sight of this formidable barrier, all but
two of the eager sportsmen prudently abate their
speed and look about them for a safe gap in the
fence. The twain more adventurous than, the rest,
or else having greater confidence in the vaulting
qualities of their steeds, keep straight ahead in
their hurrying career, fierce competitors for the
honor of being first in at the death. They are
abreast, though some paces apart. At this stage
of the sport, the looker-on from the hill fairly
brims over with excitement; but it does not appear,
from the tenor of his exclamations, that he would
have those two madcaps desist from their dare-
devil attempt.

"That's Dick Alloway on the sorrel; but who
can the other fellow be? No matter; ten to one
neither of them makes the leap. You and I could
do it, old boy," addressing his horse, which at the
moment looked the image of a "fiery Pegasus;"
"and we are the only pair in the county. By
George! they are over it. Splendid! splendid!"

Sure enough, there they were, over the fence as
clear as a whistle, and off like the wind neck and
neck for the woods, into which they soon disap-
pear. The more sober gaited of the party, having
abandoned the contest for the prize, follow on each
according to his whim. Presently, the blast of a
horn announces the catastrophe, and as its echoes

2*

die away along the hills a deeper quiet than ever
settles down upon the scene. Huntsmen and hounds
have vanished like a dream from sight and hearing,
and our traveler, recovering himself, replaces the hat
which he had snatched from his head in the excitement of the moment, gives the rein to his mettle-
some steed, and goes on his way at a bounding pace.

Crossing the ferry, a mile or so beyond the river,
just as the last rays of the sun lingered on the
tree tops, he turned off abruptly from the highway he was pursuing into the depth of a large
virgin forest. He had gone but a short way in
his new direction, when he was startled by a noise
which resembled, in thrilling intensity and prolonged horror, the war-whoop of an Indian savage;
but as the last relic of the interesting race of
yore had long ago disappeared from these once
familiar haunts, of course the sound could not be
referred to any such alarming source. Stopping
his horse, he sought an explanation of the rude
clamor which, judging by the effect on his own
nerves, had so frightened the peaceful denizens of
the silvan bowers from their propriety. He was
not long in ascertaining that it proceeded from a
pair of lusty lungs bawling away at a song with
a stentorian gusto which set at defiance all the
laws of melodious concord. The words of the
obstreperous ditty betrayed the vocalist's zest for
the noblest of manly sports. Here is a specimen,
as near as we could come at the words:

> On yonder hill there sits a hare,
> Oppressed with sorrow, grief and care,
> Because her prospects are so bare;
> Halloo, boys, halloo!

The refrain being rendered at a pitch that made
the woods to ring, and set the owls to screeching
and hooting in mocking chorus./ It was this
unearthly diapason, which might have been likened
unto the hideous yell of the lurking red devil as
he springs from his lair, and the next moment the
gleaming tomahawk hurtles through the air and
crashes into the skull of the unsuspecting way-
farer. But to our sprightly cavalier there is something irresistibly ludicrous in the mixed concourse
of diabolical sounds, and he greets the unlooked
for serenade with a loud peal of laughter. Then,
as the lines come so pat, he cannot forbear to
shout them out at the top of his voice:

"Silence, ye wolves, while Ralph to Cynthia howls;
And makes night hideous; answer him, ye owls!"

"In Saint Hubert's name, Dickon, stop your horrible racket; you have scared the 'molly-cottontails'
out of their wits." The adjuration was addressed
to the owner of the enviable lungs, who now
appeared to view in the person of another horseman coming along a bridle-path through the woods
—a big-boned, strong-limbed, young giant he was,
with such a wilderness of light-colored hair about
his face and neck that scarcely anything could be
seen of his features. So much as was visible
showed extremely prepossessing, and the careless,
free-and-easy abandon of his mien, as well as the
merry light which danced and sparkled in his
clear, blue eyes, betokened a heart which was on
the best terms with itself, and all the world
beside. He was encased in buckskin cap-a-pie, save

that he wore the stoutest of high-topped boots that ever "skelpit through dub and mire." A large silver-mounted horn hung by a cord under his arm, at his saddle bow was displayed the trophy which proclaimed him victor in the day's hunt, and a brace of fagged and foot-sore fox hounds of the genuine "black St. Hubert's breed" limped at his horse's heels.

"Why, Harry," exclaimed the newcomer, as he rode up and shook the traveler warmly by the hand, "where did you drop from; is this the way you keep promises? We looked for you to join us to-day without fail—that was your word."

"If I lived and nothing happened," replied his merry companion, whom we introduce as young Henry Carleton, of that ilk. "You may be sure it was not my fault, Dick, that I did not give you a tilt for the brush I see you have there. My father, who is just returned from Richmond, detained me all morning writing letters for him, until it was too late for me to take part in your hunt. You may see I was in trim for the fray," pointing to his nether garment.

"Well," replied Alloway, accepting his friend's explanation, "I am delighted to see you all the same, though you certainly did miss a glorious treat—just one uproarious frolic from beginning to end; men, dogs and horses perfectly frantic with delight," and with true sportman's enthusiasm, he launched forth in an animated description of the chase, as they rode on together.

"Oh, I witnessed the grand closing scene from the ferry hill," said Carleton, interrupting the flow

of Somervilian eloquence. "Tell me, who was the
spruce-looking fellow on the gallant · grey, who
seemed to be pushing you so hard for the prize?"

"Pushing me so hard? You may well say that,"
replied Alloway, "for if his horse had not tripped
over a hanging vine and tumbled the fine gentleman over its head, he would have undoubtedly
won the race by several lengths. He wasn't a
bit hurt by the fall; but you should have heard
him swear at his ; horse in the most outlandish
gibberish, as if the poor animal could help the
vine's being in the way. Who is he? That's precisely what I would like to find out; none of the
party knew anything about him. He landed among
us right out of the clouds; pitched like fury into
the sport without asking anybody's leave, and when
it was over he vanished in a flash no one saw
whither."

Carleton.—"What's he like, this terrible hobgoblin
of the chase?"

Alloway.—"Oh, good enough looking, for that
matter, if he wasn't so infernally black—I don't
mean his skin, which is none of the fairest—his
eyes and hair, especially his eyes—they looked like
two great lumps of charcoal with the light shining
through 'em, and Jupiter! how the sparks flew out
of 'em when his horse threw him—like a whole
blazing pile of hickory logs spitting fire all at
once. One thing I must say for the fellow, he
certainly knows how to sit a horse, and had he
not shown a spice of the devil in his temper, I
would have desired better acquaintance, instead of
leaving him and his horse to settle their little
misunderstanding the best way they could."

Carleton.—"Now, you have described an Italian brigand or other sort of gentleman-like cutthroat."

The big sportsman jerked up his shoulders in sign of contempt, and would have replied, doubtless, in a manner the gesture implied, had not the sharp crack of a rifle close by cut short the colloquy. At the same instant a squirrel came bounding from an overhanging limb a rod in front of them, and had barely touched the ground before a stout, half-grown stripling sprang into the road, gun in hand, and, snatching up the game, held it aloft in triumph, his face betokening the liveliest pleasure.

"Well shot, Archie," exclaimed Alloway; "from a rest, I'll wager."

"Indeed it was not, Mr. Alloway, it was a fair off-hand shot, and I did not see anything but its head, either," protested the youth, pointing to the wound behind the creature's ear.

"I only jested," replied Alloway; "it is not the first proof I have had of your marksmanship. But it is too late for another shot; come, mount behind, I am going to take you home with me."

"No, thank you, Mr. Alloway," replied the lad, "I have not been out on a regular hunt; I just came on an errand for father, and must hasten back. He says he wants you to come over early in the morning and attend to that little matter he spoke to you about several days ago; I suppose you know what it is, I am sure I do not."

"Oh, yes, I understand," said Alloway; "say to your father that I will be on hand between nine and ten o'clock, and be sure and tell your mother it was my fault that you did not get home to supper."

"Oh, I'll be there by candle-light," laughingly exclaimed the boy, as he bounded away through the woods like a deer.

"A pretty youth, Dick," said Carleton, as they resumed their journey; "who is he?"

"The very question I was asking myself for the hundredth time," replied Alloway. "Archie is a fine, manly little fellow; I wish I knew more about him."

Carleton.—"Not know who the boy is? why you seem well acquainted with his father."

Alloway.—"There's the quandary; Archie is a foster-child. If I only could muster courage to ask the collector."

Carleton.—"The collector? Pray what new riddle is that, you incorrigible sphinx?"

Alloway.—"The collector, the great exciseman, the tax-gathering plenipotentiary of our Cæsar-Augustus; who else could it be but old Jake Thompson, the most redoubtable tory inside of the capes."

Carleton.—"I have frequently heard of the eccentric Mr. Jacob Thompson, but not by that formidable designation."

Alloway.—"And you never heard how he earned the title? Ah, I remember, you were at college when it happened. Mr. Lee was addressing a large gathering of the rebellious clans at the court house, when Mr. Thompson suddenly burst in among the crowd, boiling over with indignation. He called the speaker a vile incendiary, traitor, demagogue, and the like, and warned the people not to listen to his seditious harangue. Parliament, he said, not only had the right to tax them, but ought to tax them till they groaned; it was a glorious privilege to pay tribute to such a beneficent government, and if his blessed majesty would only make him collector-general of his dominions in America, he would teach his refractory subjects a lesson of obedience to lawful authority they would not forget in a hurry. The irate gentleman soon discovered that he was in the wrong pew; he was hustled out amid a storm of yells and hoots, and it was as much as we could do to keep the populace from giving him a chairing after the vulgar fashion. From that day he has been known by a variety of nicknames, all indicating the supreme object of his loyal ambition. Here, everybody, down to the school-boys, calls him Collector Thompson, and far from resenting their familiarity, he actually glories in the popular recognition of his zeal in his royal master's service. Once in a while he breaks out and ramps and raves like all bedlam let loose; but take him right, you will find him to be at bottom a very good kind of an old heathen—doesn't bear a particle of malice, and is openhanded and honest as the day."

Carleton.—"But what has the old tory to do with the boy?"

Alloway.—"Everything—he and his wife. Having no children of their own, they have adopted Archie; but where they picked him up, I have not the remotest idea."

Carleton.—"Another Tom Jones in embryo, very likely. Come now, Dick, who do you suppose the wild huntsman to be; for to me, he is a more interesting personage than your little foundling."

Another pronounced shrug was all the reply.

Carleton.—"A brave set of fellows, truly; twenty of you to one poor forlorn foreigner, and not one had the courage to ask him a civil question. How I wish I had been there."

Alloway.—"What would you have done? most puissant imp of valor."

Carleton.—"What would I have done? Why, first of all, I would have gone to the relief of the discomfited unknown cavalier and helped him to remount; next, I would have felicitated him, in a delicate way, on his superb horsemanship, and tendered him the prize, which an untoward accident deprived him of; and, in fine, I would have genearly dispensed him the hospitable treatment which is due to a stranger and a gentleman—common politeness, nothing more. Suppose now, this terrible person should turn out to be what I verily suspect he is—"

"No more of that, Hal, an' thou lovest me," exclaimed Alloway, retreating behind an apt quotation. "And since you speak of politeness, I am reminded to say, welcome to Woodbourne, if you have been all this while paying me that long promised visit."

"There, again, my dear friend, I am not to blame," replied Carleton. "It was impossible for me to leave home while my father was absent on that plaguey Indian business; and ever since he came back he has had me constantly at work in the fourfold capacity of scribe, amanuensis, confidential secretary, and general factotem. I am only this moment relieved of my multifarious task; my

3

luggage is on the way, and you are not going to be rid of me for some days."

"Only stay until you wear your welcome out, and I will overlook past transgressions," replied Alloway, in his hearty manner.

By this time they had gotten clear of the forest, and, passing through a gateway which opened upon a wide lawn, were approaching a large and comely mansion, half hidden in a tuft of sheltering trees, and perched upon the summit of what, in that country, was regarded as a somewhat ambitious knoll. This was Woodbourne, the goodly residence of Mr. Richard Austin Alloway, where he maintained, with a very bad grace, it was said, his present reign of solitary grandeur.

CHAPTER III.

MR. RICHARD ALLOWAY'S mother was an Austin. The founder of the Virginia family of that name was the younger son of a younger brother, who appears to have drifted hither towards the close of the seventeenth century. At an early period of his life he set out from Kent County, England, to seek his fortune wheresoever he could find it, and in his case the proverb of the rolling stone received a flat contradiction. His various enterprises on land and sea met with unvarying success, and he rapidly accumulated a considerable store of wealth. Jamaica was the last field of his commercial operations. Thence he removed to Virginia, having previously invested the bulk of his large means in land and negro slaves. He now abandoned mercantile pursuits, and became a planter of magnificent proportions. From this description, it is easy to infer that Mr. Richard Austin the elder was one of those solid men of whom the saw, "Better to be born lucky than rich," was written, and who, in all the mutations of human affairs, never lose sight of the main chance nor let go an opportunity to turn an honest penny. Had he devoted himself body and soul to the service of Mammon, he would in all probability have become the reigning monarch of Change Alley, and, dying, left a pile in the funds for executorial "rooks, committee men and trustees," to squander in contingent fees and incidental expenses, to say nothing of fat salaries to countless dispensers of infinitesimal benefactions to the widow and fatherless. O, blind heaper-up of the shining hoard, why should you be so much concerned about the disposition of your toilsome gains when you yourself shall have been hutched in the insatiable grave? What difference will it make in the general account of human happiness whether

> To heirs unknown descends the unguarded store,
> Or wanders, Heaven directed, to the poor?

It was Richard Austin's son who designed the capacious dwelling that erstwhile looked down in stately pride from the crest of yonder sedgy knoll, and of which naught remains to tell the tale save a crumbling heap of bricks and mortar, and the charred end or two of a beam or rafter. It was burned by the British in the war of 1812, one of the many similar acts of vandalism of which the locality retains the proof to this day.

Mr. John Austin was liberally educated at the best schools in England, obtained a degree at Oxford, and received the extra polishing of the grand Continental tour. That he made the most of his opportunities is evident from the fact, that had he not been a man of rare talents and acquirements, he could not possibly have attained to the

honors he in after years enjoyed, having, at different
times, been a member of Council, sat several ses-
sions in the House of Burgesses, and filled, as long
as he desired it, the responsible office of Presiding
Justice and High Sheriff of the county. Under
his forming hands Woodbourne blossomed as a rose
in the wilderness, and displayed in every feature
the evidences of a cultivated mind and refined
taste. To this day the name recalls whatever of
elegant ease, solid comfort and social pleasure found
an abode within "the ancient, hospitable hall

> Whose vaulted roof once rung to harmless mirth:
> Where every passing stranger was a guest,
> And every guest a friend."

For all that the house had its skeleton. Here,
as everywhere, the stream of happiness was "the
torrent's smoothness ere it falls below." This picture of joy and gladness could not last for the
brief space of one man's life, and the last days of
Mr. John Austin's career on earth repeat the sad,
sad story of the vanity of human wishes. He had
but one son, the youngest of seven children, and
although he was far from wanting affection for
his daughters, the boy had been the principal
object of his pride and care. The good dominie
who held the station of private tutor in the family
was not permitted to have exclusive control of his
pupil's training. The fond father devoted every
leisure moment to the grateful task, and deemed
himself abundantly rewarded for his diligent pains.
The boy was sprightly, apt and ambitious to learn,
and not only did he master with ease the lessons

3*

which were assigned him, but by the time he was seventeen years old he had read through every book of travel, history and polite literature in his father's well-stored library, and thus acquired an amazing deal of miscellaneous information. With these advantages he was sent to the college at Williamsburg, and it was intended, when he had taken the course there, he should complete his studies abroad.

In the bright annals of the Old Dominion there is no name of purer lustre than that of Commissary Blair, the pioneer of letters, to whom belongs the imperishable honor of having erected a temple where all the wisdom of the old world Egyptians could be had without encountering the perils and cost of a double voyage across the ocean. His darling foster-child was now grown to be a flourishing seminary of science and literature. In another decade it became the prolific nursery of republican genius, the fountain to which the brightest intellects of the colony repaired, and "in their golden urns drew light."

Thoroughly accoutred by previous careful preparation, Richard Austin enlisted with the fairest auspices in the earnest and jealous contests of his new arena. Among his associates were a score of ardent competitors, all eager to endure the suffocating heat and dust of the Olympic course to win the victor's crown of glory. Naturally, his disposition was the most amiable and gentle; he was ingenuous, frank and warm-hearted to a fault, and the current of his feelings and affections usually flowed in a strong, even and pellucid channel. Whilst he was a general favorite with his fellow-students, he had especially singled out one among the number for his warmest and most intimate regard, and this attachment gradually ripened into a friendship passing the love of women.

The session was drawing to a close; the final examinations were close at hand, and the candidates for the various badges of merit vied with each other in unremitting application to their absorbing duties. Foremost in the generous race were Richard Austin and his friend, Reginald Aubrey, twin stars in the galaxy of academic distinction. In the midst of the animated contest, a marked change was observed in Richard's deportment; he grew suddenly morose and cynical, neglected his books, and went moping about in solitary despondency. One evening, while the spell was on him, he was crossing the college campus, where a number of students were playing at cricket, when one of them thoughtlessly accosted him in what he conceived to be an insulting and jeering manner. Instantly he stooped, and, seizing a large stone, threw it with all his strength at the offender's head. The deadly missile flew harmlessly past the mark at which it was aimed, to find a dearer victim, and striking poor Aubrey full upon the temple, felled him to the earth. The blow was fatal. Let us not linger on the harrowing story. The anguish and remorse of the unhappy young man were terrible beyond description; and when his father came to take him home, his sorrowful companions could scarcely recognize, in the stony image of voiceless and tearless woe around which they stood weeping, a trace of the once light-

hearted leader of their sportive pastimes, and many
wondered if it were not better to be with him
whom they had tenderly laid to rest in the silent
grave. Ah, could he have whispered one little
word, or had he even smiled in his sleep when
the cry of wild, despairing agony burst from the
wretched form that bent over him as he lay so
cold and still upon the ground! Alas! there was
no solacing remembrance—no transient gleam of
compassion—no drop of healing balm in the overflowing cup of hopeless misery. Like a plummet
the soul of Reginald Aubrey dropped into the
ocean of eternity, and from that moment Richard
Austin was rarely ever seen to smile.

Thus it happened that one flash of an angry
spirit had kindled a fire which consumed to ashes
as fair a temple as was ever fashioned by skill
divine. O, wretched man, voyager on life's uncertain main, be not beguiled into false security because
the sea is calm and the stars are shining brightly
over your head. In calm and storm alike be ever
watchful and circumspect. To the wary pilot the
ripple on the glassy surface gives warning of the
jagged reef that lurks below. Let that strong
hand for an instant loose its hold upon the helm,
and the frail vessel which bears your soul's eternal
fortunes is engulphed in the yawning deep, or
drifts, a shattered and helpless wreck on the bosom
of the remorseless wave. Beware! beware! or else
learn, when it is too late, that to the mind which
is not already callous grown in sin there may
come an anguish which cannot be wearied down,
a pang which cannot be assuaged.

For weeks the grief of Richard Austin was excessive, and manifested itself in such fearful convulsions that his father inwardly prayed for death to come and release him from suffering. At length these violent paroxysms ceased entirely, and were succeeded by another form of malady, less poignant in the excruciating torture of the body, but distressing beyond measure, inasmuch as it foreshadowed the worst calamity which could befall the unhappy youth. He sunk into a deep, pervading, listless melancholy; a thick, impenetrable pall of gloomy dejection shrouded his whole being; it was the acme of the misery which "rejoiceth exceedingly, and is glad when it can find the grave." Hour after hour he sat, silent and motionless, gazing on vacancy, and when he was with difficulty pursuaded to move at all, he walked with uncertain and tottering steps, as one whose senses were completely dazed and who had lost the faculty of volition. The family physician now gravely shook his head, and frankly confessed that his patient was beyond the reach of any remedy he possessed. There was but one recourse left, he said, which promised a chance of success. He had known a change of air and scene to prove efficacious in similar disorders after the ordinary appliances of medical skill had been exhausted in vain. The advice was taken. To his father's great joy, Richard yielded readily to his entreaties, and they set out on a voyage to England. The result showed the value of Dr. Harrington's prescription. The trip across the ocean of itself wrought a miracle of cure, which Mr. Austin had not dared to hope for; there was a precious elixir in the far-sweeping breezes unknown to human science, and when they reached their destination Richard was so far restored to health as to evince a lively interest in the unaccustomed sights and scenes around him. In a little while the cloud which hung upon his mind slowly lifted and floated away, and the light shone out again. But not with the radiance of its early beams. It was no longer the glory of the sun, sparkling with myriad hues of ever-changing brightness; but a soft, dreamy and subdued influence of moon and stars, as of a halo from another world. The beautiful visions of life's morning march, the glowing aspirations for worldly fame and rewards, the fairy forms and fantasies of young desire, each object of passionate love and eager anticipation, which had imparted energy and animation to his heart, appeared through the mystic drapery of that serene shadowy twilight of the soul, like an unsubstantial pageant fast fading from sight. The old vivacity and humor, the bounding pulse, the elastic step, the gay, soaring spirit were gone, and instead of these was a quiet, sedate, earnest and contemplative demeanor, as if the mind was constantly occupied with dark communings on subjects of everlasting import. This was, indeed, the very crisis of his fate. A deadly blight had fallen upon his prospects and fame. He had no pleasure in the diversions where happiness is usually sought. His heart was a fountain of bitter waters, and despair presented its poisoned chalice to his lips. But thanks to his early complete religious training, he, in this supreme moment of mortal agony, turned a deaf ear to the voice of the tempter, and taking up his heavy cross bore it with unmurmuring patience to the end.

Richard Austin had remained abroad scarcely a year, when he was summoned home by the illness of his father. Here he arrived in time to close the dying eyes of his only parent, and a few months afterwards he was called upon to perform the same sad task in the case of the unmarried oldest sister, who had been to him from infancy in the place of the mother he had never seen. Of his remaining sisters, Mrs. Alloway alone resided in the vicinity of Woodbourne; the others were scattered far and wide over the colony. All of them were happily married, and did not require his aid and protection. So, having arranged his affairs, and given all needful instructions to his overseer, he locked up the house, handed the key to the faithful old butler, and once again crossed the Atlantic, this time to become an aimless and solitary wanderer in foreign lands. He left an address with Mrs. Alloway where letters would reach him, but he did not answer one of the many which she, with true sisterly affection, continued to write all the same as though he had been the most punctual of correspondents.

Years rolled by, and still no tidings came from him, nor could the persistent inquiries of the friends who, from time to time, visited Europe discover the faintest trace of his footsteps. His secret was known to but two bosoms, by whom it was held in the close embrace of professional confidence—that of the old lawyer who had been his father's most intimate friend and counsellor in his private and public affairs, and of his agent in London.

Mrs. Alloway went regularly to Woodbourne four or five times a year to make a thorough inspection of the premises, and especially to see that the flowers were properly cared for, and the fruit trees did not suffer for want of pruning. To her the old place was always home, and nowhere else did the roses and dahlias bloom so gorgeously, nor the plums and apricots hang with such tempting lusciousness. On these visits she was accompanied by the children, in whose eyes grandfather's house, as they called it, was a miracle of magnificence, which laughed Aladdin's palace to scorn. What a merry sight it was, to see these little elves drop suddenly from the clouds, and put to rout the legions of grim spectres lurking there in that sombre and forsaken abode. How they scampered through the house, chased around the lawn, tumbled over the flower-beds, climbed the cherry trees, swung upon the garden gate, ransacked the poultry yard, performed every imaginable mischievous antic, and raised such a din about the ears of Uncle George Hamilton, the sable factotum in charge, that he wished them a thousand times in Jericho, and wondered what Miss Jane could have been thinking about to fetch them there to "towse and mummock things to pieces that sort o' way." But Miss Jane did not pay the slightest attention to the grand airs of her brother's prime minister, and the children gamboled on in unrebuked gleefulness.

Master Richard Austin Alloway was now a great,

gawky, hobble-de-hoy urchin, with a freckled face, a tangled shock of sandy hair, a small flock of goslings in his voice, and a superabundance of good humor and animal spirits. He had learned to ride and shoot, to fish and hunt, and to swim like a duck, to bridle a three-year old, and break him, too, to worm a dog, and phlegm a horse—in a word, he was a very prince of the tribe of Nimrod, and the Admirable Crichton of rustic accomplishments. Of the nectared sweets of learning, he does appear to have been particularly fond, being like other truants given to exclaim, *jam satis*, before testing the fact whether crude surfeit reigned in repletion. In Latin, Cæsar's bridge was an everlasting stumbling block, and as for Greek, the very alphabet was the quintessence of foolishness. But although he was not on speaking terms with the heroes of Homer and Virgil, he was well up in English history, and had by heart the entire catalogue of British celebrities, from Boadicea, warlike queen, to Captain James Cook, the latest wonder of the world. Moreover, he knew perfectly well that the world was round like a ball, and not flat, like a pan-cake; that the old turn and turn about theory was all gammon, and that the earth revolved on its own "axle-tree" once in twenty-four hours, and circumgyrated round the sun in three hundred and sixty-five days and a fraction over, which explained all about night and day, and winter and summer, and led to the invention of the mariner's compass and the discovery of America! Add to the list a familiar acquaintance with the exploits of "Jack-the-Giant-Killer," the wonders of the

4

"Arabian Nights," the adventures of "Robinson Crusoe," and such knowledge of the Episcopal catechism as a pious mother's unremitting care did not fail to supply, and this inventory of Master Dick's then acquirements is well nigh complete.

The fields and forests of Woodbourne were a favorite resort of this young poacher, and if, which was rarely the case, he did not succeed in filling his game-bag, he was sure to come back with his pockets groaning with the spoils of the orchard. There were no interdicted preserves in this part of the colony, and the sportsman was free to roam and ravage at will; yet there was an illusion of forbidden pleasure to Richard in thus trespassing on his uncle's domain, from the fact that it was highly displeasing to the august functionary we have spoken of, who looked upon it as an offence, nothing short of *leze majestie* to shoot a squirrel in the gum-spring woods!

One day, towards the end of the month of October, 1770, Richard had started with his gun and dog on one of these predatory excursions to Woodbourne, saying, as usual, that they might not look for him before supper time. He had been gone but a few hours, when he came hurriedly back in a great flurry of excitement, and startled his mother with the intelligence that he had seen a strange person walking on the lawn, and had stood and watched him ever so long, and saw him go across to the graveyard and pull one of the flowers she said nobody was to touch, and how he was dressed in a rich suit of black velvet and walked with a cane, and seemed to be weak and lame, and—well,

that was all. He had run every step of the way to
let her know about it. Who could the stranger
be?

"Your own dear uncle, my son," replied the good
lady, warmly embracing the bearer of the joyful
news. "There, run and order the carriage to be
brought, and send some one for your father." And
in the next hour Mr. Alloway and his wife were
rolling rapidly along the road to Woodbourne.

To the desolate wanderer the meeting was unspeak-
ably affecting, and he wept and sobbed on his
sister's breast in a wild, passionate way, which
showed how, in all the days of his dreary pilgrimage, his heart was ever yearning for that one touch
of heavenly sympathy. Where he had been, what
he had been doing, and how he had fared, none
ever heard the whole story from his lips. He seldom referred to his personal adventures, and seemed
to regard whatever had befallen him as of no consequence to the rest of the world. There was
neither affectation of indifference nor ill-natured
reticence in this enforced silence; only the weariness of melancholy dejection, and blank, unfathomed
desolation of heart. Not a murmur of complaint
nor symptom of impatience escaped him in word
or gesture; still, the bent form, the tottering gait,
the worn and weary look, and wan and wasted
features, these told their eloquent tale of sorrow
and suffering, and showed that at all times and in
all places the ceaseless horror, "fell tyrant of the
throbbing breast," held its victim bound with an
iron chain. Every trace of angry passion and cynical emotion had departed; he was now all gentle-

ness and patience and holy resignation, watching
and waiting for the joyful summons which would
call the grief-burdened soul to its appointed rest.
Such was his appearance to the observant eyes of
his affectionate sister, when the first gush of suppressed feeling was over and he had relapsed into
his habitual seriousness. Her womanly intuition
divined the secret at a glance, and she felt a thrill
of unspeakable rapture on finding that all was well
with him at home. He had sought and found the
Peace which the world cannot give nor take away.

Mrs. Alloway came to see him every day for
weeks after his return, and found him always the
same quiet, uncomplaining and abstracted being. To
her anxious inquiries after his health, he invariably
responded that he slept well, felt no decided pain,
and usually ate with a relish what was set before
him. On one of these visits she was much gratified to observe that he noticed the absence of the
children, and wondered why they were never brought
to see him; so far from being annoyed by them,
nothing she could devise would afford him half so
much agreeable diversion as their merry gambols and
innocent prattle. After that they always accompanied her, and frequently came by themselves. At
first they were considerably awed in his presence, but
they were not long in finding out that he was the
gentlest and most harmless of God's creatures,
instead of the terrible ogre they had been led to
imagine from the mystery in which his history
was enveloped. In a little while his grave deportment ceased to impress them; but what they lacked
in reverence, they more than made up in fondness.

And now the master was here, even the frowning grimaces and dreadful contortions of old George the butler, began to lose their former terrors. "Uncle didn't care," was the aggravating reply to every protestation of the enraged majordomo; "and everything on the land belonged to uncle, himself in the bargain; and he was nothing but an ugly, black, *Guinea* nigger, for all his consequential airs," which sally of juvenile wit never failed to rout the enemy, horse, foot and dragoons. Matters were even worse than before he came home, and the disgusted old servant, himself a paragon of all that was proper and decorous in behavior, out of patience with such weakness, wishes he had staid away altogether, since he was of no more account in his own house than to be made a stick-horse of by "dem audacious chill'un of Miss Jane's," the mention of whom was always coupled with the awful prognostication that "de debble was sartin to git de las' one on 'em." The monster! couldn't he see that the boisterous romps and antics of this wild troup of joyous sprites was worth all the physic in Dr. Harrington's saddle-bags to his master, and brought the only ray of real cheerfulness that ever illumined that sad face? And when they gathered around his chair, under the spreading oak on the lawn, to listen with breathless interest to the voice so unlike any they had heard before in its strangely plaintive and musical tones, telling such beautiful stories of the far-off lands he had visited, and the wonderful people and things he had seen, his devoted sister overflowed with thankfulness to find her tender ministering was not unavailing, since it

4*

awakened in his breast transitory gleams of sunshine which she feared would never revisit that shady desert.

Shortly after his uncle's return, Richard was sent from home to try what efficacy there was in a noted fountain of learning in an adjoining county. To what extent he partook of its Pierian waters, and whether he derived any great benefit from the same, we have not been able to ascertain; but from the fact that he was never heard to brag of his attainments, it may be safely conjectured that he was contented with the intoxicating effect of shallow draughts, and left to older topers the sober delights of potations pottle deep. When his vacation came, Mr. Austin, who had manifested much interest in the boy, importuned his father to let him come and live at Woodbourne. Mr. Alloway readily consented, and as Dick was now grown almost to be a man, his society and assistance became at once a source of unmistakable pleasure and comfort to the lonely occupant of the great mansion, who, among other things, now directed his studies, and succeeded in inspiring him with a relish of the dainties which are bred in a book which he had never before experienced. With the help of such a kind and affectionate mentor, he made wonderful progress, and well-nigh atoned for his misspent hours. In return, he gave his attention to the affairs of the plantation, and as he did not interfere with Uncle George's department, everything went on now as pleasantly as could be desired by all parties. In and about the house was a perpetual atmosphere of calm serenity and tranquil repose, now and then disturbed by an incursion of the old butler's uproarious tormentors. Apparently, Mr. Richard Austin was greatly improved in health and spirits; yet he never went into society, and, except an occasional visit to his sister, led a life of perfect retirement and seclusion. His nephew relieved him of the irksome cares of his estate, and was the almoner of his generous bounty to the poor, so that he was wholly exonerated from worldly concerns. But he marked how swiftly the days were gliding by, and knew that his end was fast approaching.

One morning last May, Richard, who had been on some unusual errand, came in late to breakfast, and was surprised to find his uncle had not yet made his appearance. He was an early riser, and it was his custom, when dressed, to go to his library and spend an hour in study and devotion. Here they found him kneeling beside a chair, his head bowed over his clasped hands, which rested on the Holy Book he had opened for the last time. His prayer was answered; the poor captive was free, and the sweet smile which lingered on his face, recalling the image of his boyish grace and beauty, showed with what blissful ecstacy he had greeted the messenger of Heaven, and walked with him out of the dark shadow into the light of eternal happiness. His grave is the fourth one you see there, and the fifth is that of the old slave who followed him in a little while, and was laid at the feet of those he had so long and faithfully served. Such was the peaceful close of a life which had been embittered by one crushing grief, and it was consoling to know that during the last years of his earthly sojourn he had found an alleviation of his sorrows.

By his uncle's will, which was written before he went abroad, and lodged with Mr. Copland, the old lawyer whom we have mentioned, and which was never afterwards altered, his nephew succeeded to all his property, and as he left no debts or legacies to be paid, there was nothing to do but to take immediate possession without legal formalities of any description. And thus we find Mr. Richard Austin Alloway, at the free age of one-and-twenty, lord of the goodly manor of Woodbourne, with all its broad acres of field and forest—as fine a specimen of a free-handed, bold-spirited, bluff and burly country squire as could be found in the wide borders of the Old Dominion; a noted fox hunter, to be sure, and the proud owner of the winner of the sweepstakes at Mt. Airy race-field; yet by no means the embodiment of extravagance, idleness and dissipation, which he is represented to be in the caricaturing pictures of certain prejudiced and prudish story writers. He is very popular with his neighbors, young and old; entertains as becomes his station and fortune, and makes one in every party for pleasure and amusement; but he does not, on any account, neglect his plantation, which he manages without the aid of an overseer, and his affairs prosper accordingly. For the rest, it is evident that he does not intend to remain a bachelor longer than he can help, and of late the frequent apparition of a stalwart cavalier on a well-known sorrel horse, with a nosegay at his button·

hole, and a countenance expressive of the extremes
of sheepish bashfulness and reckless indifference,
always going the self-same way, furnishes an exhaust-
less theme for gossiping people, who will persist
in taking so much trouble upon themselves about
matters that don't concern them. How his wooing
sped will in due time appear.

CHAPTER IV.

TO resume the thread of our story, the young gentlemen from whom we parted a moment ago to take this short flight over the "dark backward and abysm of time," are now seated by a cheerful fire in the dining-room; for, although the days are remarkably mild for the season, the nights are so cool that the warm blaze does not come amiss in that spacious apartment. Dick has been telling about his uncle, and when he had finished his voice was tremulous, and a tear was glistening in his mild, blue eye. His friend was far from being unmoved by the touching story, and sat for some time in deep meditation, gazing intently at the fire as if it were a Merlin's Mirror, in which he expected to find an explanation of all that is dark and enigmatical in human life.

"Dick," he at length said, musingly, "I hope you will not think me impertinent for pursuing a delicate topic—your family secrets—but there is a mystery here I would like to explore."

Dick.—"Certainly not, Harry; you are heartily welcome to all the information I have to impart; but, really, I am unable to see what there is so very mysterious in my poor uncle's sorrowful history."

Harry.—"Nothing in the history, as far as it is written; but were you never curious to learn what was in the books the sybil burned? You are quite sure he left no record of his travels?"

Dick.—"None, as far as I have discovered in examining his papers; not the remotest hint of anything that happened to him while he was abroad is divulged in his writings, and all I know of the matter is what he told me at odd times, when in the vein of talking. The reason why the efforts to find his retreat proved futile, is now perfectly obvious—he had changed his name in order to prevent the possibility of his being traced. Doubtless, he imagined that this self-imposed penitence would be of no avail, unless it was fulfilled with scrupulous severity."

Harry.—"Was the late Mr. Austin a Roman Catholic?"

Dick.—"On the other hand, he was ardently attached to the Church of England; why do you ask?"

Harry.—"You spoke of his doing penance, which, as you know, is a word of fearful significance to devout Catholics—means frightful torturings and macerations of the flesh, lacerating integuments, horrible flagellations, peas and pebbles in one's shoes, sackcloth and ashes, pierced with cold, tormented with hunger, parched with thirst, and ever so many other unimaginable and unendurable agonies. Did he suffer all or any of these things?"

Dick.—"Of course I did not mean that sort of

penance. Indeed, I only used the word for want of a better. From the time that I came to know him well, he was religiously abstemious and self-denying, a pattern of temperance in all respects; but I am sure he did not entertain the fanatical notion, that the troubles of the mind could be eased or dispelled by racking the body with every manner of pain. Whenever the children came to see him, he would talk to them for hours at a time, in a pleasant and instructive way, of his ramblings and observations in Europe, and his sketches of characters and scenes were often exquisitely racy and humorous; especially glowing and beautiful was the description he gave them, with almost childish rapture, of what he called his 'Happy Valley,' in Switzerland, where he lived a whole year in a family of the better class of peasantry, for whom he formed the strongest attachment. Our conversation was usually confined to literary, moral and religious topics, followed by critical remarks from him on his favorite authors. He was thoroughly versed in French and Italian, and had what seemed to me to be an inordinate passion for Tasso, from whose 'Jerusalem Delivered' I trust to be evermore excused. That and 'Milton's Paradise Lost' were the toughest jobs I ever undertook; but to please Uncle Richard, I went resolutely through both of them without skipping a line."

Harry.—"Which is more than I can say. Is that all, Dick?"

Dick.—"Yes; at least I can think of nothing more at present."

Harry.—"One other question—but no, I will not

trouble you with that." Then suddenly putting on a quizzical mask of profound gravity, he continued, quoting from the quaint old Knight of Norwich: "'What songs the syrens sung, or what name Achilles assumed when he hid himself among women, though puzzling questions, are not beyond all conjecture.' My bay against your sorrel, Dickon, that I unmask your domino the very first trial. Your uncle's name--his assumed one, that is to say—was Metcalf."

Alloway regarded his companion with undisguised amazement.

"Why, Harry," he exclaimed, "you are—"

"Doctor Faustus or the devil!" cried his lively companion. "Don't be alarmed, old fellow; there is not a grain of black magic in it. Strange, though," he muttered, as if talking to himself, "that this interesting *solitaire* should never have occurred to us to be the man we were looking for."

Dick.—"The man you were looking for? What in the name of common sense do you mean by this provoking mummery?"

Harry (still preserving his serio-comic vein).— "*Davus sum non Œdipus;* you can read the riddle for yourself. Hearken unto the story. Some four or five months ago, while the convention was sitting, there came to Richmond a stranger, whose unusual appearance and mysterious behavior created no little stir in political circles. He brought letters from Mr. Charles Carroll, of Maryland, to Mr. Peyton Randolph and other distinguished gentlemen, to whom he made known his business, and then disappeared as quietly as he came. What was

the nature of his communication has not yet
exactly transpired, but report says it had an important bearing on the questions at issue with
Great Britain. The general notion seemed to be
that he was a secret ambassador of the French
Court. Shortly after his visit, the exigency of
public affairs called my father to the temporary
capital, where, meeting with Mr. Randolph, he was
casually asked by that gentleman whether he was
acquainted with a man in Virginia named Richard
Metcalf, and answering to a particular description.
His late visitor, said he, was greatly concerned to
discover the whereabouts of the person he had
described, and he had engaged to look him up if
he could be found in the colony. My father had
never heard of such an individual, but promised
to aid Mr. Randolph in searching for him. All
inquiries up to the time of Mr. Randolph's sudden death were fruitless, and after that lamentable
event my father gave himself no further concern
about the matter, until he received a letter from
Mr. Carroll, some days ago, repeating the inquiry.
The stranger, I learned, was a Catholic priest, the
Abbé Julian Soulé. Did you ever hear of the
name?"

Alloway shook his head; he was sorely puzzled.
"It is too hard a nut for me to crack, Harry;
a Catholic priest? What could he possibly want
with Uncle Richard?"

"Yes, a veritable Catholic priest," repeated his
friend, resuming his rallying tone; "you could not
well look more preposterously horrified if I had
said it was Old Nick himself, in hot pursuit of

some poor forsworn wretch who had managed to give him the slip, having repented too late of an evil bargain with the arch-enemy. Nonsense, Dick; you know well enough your good uncle was not a sorcerer, nor, what some folks think a great deal worse, a papist. I thought you were superior to such vulgar prejudices."

Dick.—"You are quite in the right for so thinking; I am not the least bit prejudiced on that score. Had you said he was a Jew or a Turk, it would have made no difference, as far as uncle was concerned; his religious faith was as rooted as that oak tree out there. A Catholic priest," he slowly repeated; "yes, I remember, in that thrilling story he narrated, a priest figures conspicuously, but his name was Father Manso, an Italian; the other name, I am positively certain, I never heard before."

Carleton.—"Well, I don't reckon it is of much consequence to you and me who his reverence is, or what he is after; so, letting him go for the present with a *pax robiscum*, or what you please, tell me now, in few words, what you think is likely to be the be all and end all of this disturbance with England?"

Dick.—"That is what I would rather you should tell me, Harry; you have been playing statesman of late, and are deep in the public counsels. To my unsophisticated mind, there is every indication of a bloody and devastating civil war. It is not our fault, to be sure; we have had sufficient provocation, in all conscience, to justify an appeal to arms; but the alternative is none the less dreadful for that reason, nor will the righteousness of our cause avert the miseries which fratricidal strife is sure to entail upon us. The die is cast; the sword only can decide the quarrel; resistance to the death should now be the watchword and reply in every patriot's mouth."

Harry (eagerly).—"Just what I expected to hear from your lips; they belied you, who said you were lukewarm in the cause."

Dick (with considerable warmth).—"What right has anybody to say that of me? Because I keep my own counsel, and don't choose to go swaggering and ranting about the country like a fantastical Armido or blustering Bobadil, ravished with the music of my own valorous tongue? It is nevertheless true, I am no Hotspur."

Harry.—"All the better for that; it is a name of unlucky omen—a splendid meteor, vanishing in darkness and dismay; a spasm of heedless insurrection expiring in a field of Shrewsbury. Cool heads and stout hearts are what we need. You are right; we cannot shut out the truth by holding up our hands in hopeless deprecation. It is now either independence or abject slavery. There is no longer room for temporizing expedients and patch-work compromises. There is but one course left for us, the *ultima ratio;* and that signifies everlasting liberty, or endless subjugation to the American people. So say the oldest and most cautious heads in the colony. The fact is, my dear friend,' he proceeded to say, warming with the exciting theme, "our English cousins have never had the slightest idea of granting our very reasonable demand. They steadily look upon us as a set of political Pariahs and Ishmaelites—aliens from the Israel of British freedom, having no part or lot in the glorious heritage of Magna Charta. They have the monopoly of the commodity of price, and they mean to keep it if they can. Picture these lords of humankind, as they modestly call themselves, with their proud ports and defiant eyes passing in grand review before the nations, every dirty tatterdemalion among them swaggering about his birthright of liberty, and we, miserable outcasts from the pale of the constitution, not permitted to feed upon the husks that are left by the swinish multitude. Oh, it makes my blood boil to think of their audacious effrontery. How I wish I had never been born a British subject; a fig for the name!"

This sudden outburst of indignation was too much for Alloway's gravity. Seeing Carleton pause for breath, he caught up the satirical strain: "Let us have another manifesto of non-intercourse, Harry, and make its provisions as broad and general as the casing air. Henceforth homespun is the only wear, 'Sainte Croix' and 'Old Madeira' the only tipple; and John Bull shall not have our tobacco at a guinea a sneeze. That's the sum tottle o' the whole business—a mere matter of barter and exchange with these voracious sharks—a rump of pickled blue beef from the royal shambles for a cwt. of Virginia smoked venison; a cask of rotten Scotch herrings—"

Harry.—"Psha! those are mere trifles compared with the one great grievance—"

Dick (refusing to yield the floor).—"And then

5*

we must keep on paying the old woman over there
her annuity of pin-money for sending her Redcoats
over here to stir up the redskins to mutiny and
rage, and on no account forget to tickle the Pope
of England's nose with a tythe's pig's tail for
teaching us how to read the thirteenth chapter of
Romans backwards. Others may do what they like,
but, as for me, I hereby forever abjure, renounce,
repudiate, scorn and despise the whole race of John
Bull—not excepting Shakespeare and Spenser, and
Milton and Pope, and Bacon, and Locke and New-
ton, and Boyle and—'O, Jemmy Thompson, Jemmy
Thompson, O!'—let me not forget to anathematize
the panegyrist who lauded his mighty countrymen
after that disgustingly fulsome fashion—

> For every virtue, every worth renowned;
> Sincere, plain-hearted, hospitable, kind;
> Yet, like the mustering thunder, when provoked.
> The dread of tyrants, and the sole resource
> Of those who under grim oppression groan.

You have not forgotten my famous piece of declamation, Harry; how robustiously I used to mouth
it, to the admiration of our dear old master, rest
his soul! from 'Heavens! what a goodly prospect
spreads around,' to the awful *eidolon* of—'Public
zeal, ever musing on the common weal, and labor-
ing glorious for some great design.' Jupiter! how
fine I thought it was!—the very sublime of heroic
verse, outstripping 'Achille's Wrath' and throwing
'*Arma Virumque*' completely in the shade. Pah!
nothing but downright flummery and arrant balder-
dash from beginning to end! Oh, the luxury of
hating! I never knew what it was until now.

See how you have set me in a blaze, you firebrand of treason."

"Then," said Carleton, laughing, "I had better strike while the iron is hot. It is my purpose to go to work right away and raise a troop of light horse, and I want your assistance at the start."

Dick.—"You shall have it, heart and hand."

Harry.—"Seriously?"

Dick.—"As a Quaker at a love feast. I never jest on that subject."

Harry (enthusiastically).—"I am overjoyed to have you second my project so warmly. We will about it at once. Our noble chief shall not have cause longer to reproach us for our tardiness. As you say, it is not a subject for idle jest or vaporing. We should prepare in real earnest for the contest, and to fight we must have an army."

Dick.—"An army? Where is the army of General Washington?"

Harry.—"Little better than a mob, and fast melting away, from all accounts. We cannot fight British regulars with raw militia with any hope of success. You are a crack shot and a capital rider, my boy; but to cut a squirrel's head off with a rifle and jump a horse over a worm fence, desirable accomplishments as they may be, are not everything that is required to make a soldier of a man. Discipline, subordination, endurance, courage, fortitude—these are the necessary elements of an efficient army. It must be taught to move like a perfect machine at the will of its commander; and, fighting or retreating, marching or countermarching—"

Dick.—"Never mind the 'disciplines of the wars,' brave captain; Braddock's defeat has not shaken my faith in cold steel and steady valor. Close up, touch elbows, eyes front, march straight into the cannon's mouth, like an embattled stone wall, and—'Our army *swore* terribly in Flanders,' quoth my Uncle Toby—which last accomplishment is easily learned. It is a stubborn fact, Hal; there is no more dangerous animal alive than that same British Lion when he shakes his yellow mane and glowers and roars in very anger. It will require all the strength of our united hearts and hands, and other help beside, I am thinking, to keep our heads out of his ugly mouth. What do you perpend shall be done?"

Harry.—"Were all the people of my mind, they would declare George Washington military dictator, and resolve to a man to follow him blindfold. As it is, I shall endeavor, unfledged stripling as our reverend seniors call me, to do my full duty—carry out the scheme I have suggested, with your aid, and be ready to take the field before the campaign opens next spring. We shall have our hands full, without doubt; and, between us, Dick, matters are not as they should be at Boston. We need not proclaim our weakness on the housetops. If we did, we were irretrievably ruined—an easy prey for your ravening beast. Still the truth should not be concealed from those whose hearts are in the cause, and who have the will and the power to remedy the evil. Washington's confidential letters reveal a picture of poltroonery, sordid meanness and flagrant peculation which would be incredible if drawn by a less scrupulous pen. He calls upon the flower of the native chivalry, the real yoemanry of the land, to come to the rescue; men who will freely take upon themselves the solemn vow of consecration to the holy work, and not quit the field until their country takes her equal station among the powers of the earth. It was well enough to advertise the world of the nature and extent of our grievances; to tell King George in good, set phrase that we will not longer bear the yoke of vassalage to the mother country. Now, silence in the ranks. No more brave words; no more paper fulminations; no more exuberant outpourings of the *dulce et decus* spirit in cataracts of rhetorical bombast. Are we earnest patriots, who look upon liberty as a jewel above price? Then let us take our stand without delay in the deadly breach, by the side of our chosen leader. But we will talk further of this another time. There is a ship lying below; can you tell me anything of her movements—when she sails and whither bound?"

Dick.—"That, sir, is the good bark *Katrine*, from Glasgow, Hamilton & Osborn, owners. She is here, I am told, to take on board the household goods and chattels, Lares and Penates, of Mr. Thomas Osborn, one of the firm, who has prudently determined to go back to Scotland and stay there until the storm blows over, if not for the rest of his days. Non-intercourse has already rendered the occupation of the Scotch merchants comparatively worthless, and some of them are seeking safer and more profitable investments."

Harry.—"What of your neighbor, Mr. Graeme? How is he affected by these troubles?"

Dick.—"Generally reserved and circumspect; avoids discussion, and keeps strict guard over his temper when the behavior of certain of his countrymen in Maryland is denounced. Yet he openly avows his abhorrence of Dunmore's brutal proclamation, and declares that it and other outrages, that spring-gun affair particularly, are past endurance. Like many others, I suspect he earnestly deprecates having to resort to extreme measures, without well seeing how they can be honorably avoided. His son is as outspoken a rebel as Patrick Henry, and had to be shipped over to Scotland to keep him out of mischief. Really, though, it was done more to relieve his · mother's anxiety of mind than because his father disapproved his sentiments. By the way, Mr. Graeme can give you the information you desire respecting the vessel. He was once a partner of Mr. Osborn, and, I believe, still retains an interest in the concern.

Harry.—"Which is all the better for my purpose. Will you go with me to see him to-morrow?"

Dick.—"Yes, in the evening; I have an engagement will occupy the entire forenoon. A plague on't! I wish they had pitched on somebody else for the disagreeable job."

Harry.—"What is it, Dick?"

Dick. —"Oh, a most weighty affair. You see, my especial friend and pitcher, the collector, has been ever so long at loggerheads with an equally crossgrained neighbor about a patch of alder brake, which a fastidious muskrat wouldn't have as a gracious gift. There has been an interminable suit in ejectment between them, and at last, sick of

the law's delay, and sicker still of the fee bills
they have had to foot, they, for a wonder, agreed
to take it out of court, and refer it to two disin-
terested and judicious freeholders to decide. Lastly,
the arbitrators have locked horns, and, worse to
embroil the fray, have called me in as umpire. Do
you know what I mean to do?"

Harry.—"Halve the loaf between the litigants?"

Dick.—"No."

Harry.—"Give them an equal share apiece of
hard crust, and decree the rest in costs? that's
English for equity."

Dick.—"Not a bit of it."

Harry.—"What then, O, learned judge?"

Dick.—"Why, I intend to award the whole of
it to the frogs for a free commonwealth—a new
Atlantis, where they may croak and croak from
daylight to dawn again, with none to molest or
make them afraid."

Carleton laughed heartily. "Capital, famous," he
exclaimed; "the two-edged sword of justice cutting
both ways at once—one edge lopping off an everlasting *casus belli* between two tough old sticklers
for their rights; the other carving out a perpetual
paradise for the subjects of King Log. If you
wield a sabre with the same address, what a trooper
you will make. Then you can't go till evening;
well, that will be time enough for my business
with Mr. Graeme. I'm sorry his son is gone away;
the country can ill afford to spare such as he. Is
young Graeme their only child?

Dick—"The only son living; they had another
and—a daughter," there was just the least

tremor of embarrassment in his voice, and the faintest shade of heightened color suffused his sunburnt cheek, but they did not escape the quick, sparkling eyes of his sprightly guest.

"And one fair daughter," he exclaimed; "I see it all now; you sly old fox, earthed at last. But how is this, Dick; what have you done with your other charmer of whom report tells—the lovely rose of Clifton? she that is said to be 'the shop of all the qualities that man loves woman for.' Has the fair Roseline found a Juliet in the daisy of Bonhill? Why, I took you for the very north star of constancy, and, lo! you are as fickle as the moon. Come, unbosom; I am dying to hear—"

"Get out with your nonsense, Harry," replied the persecuted swain; "it is time to go to bed." And without further ceremony he snatched up a candle and conducted Carleton to his apartment for the night.

CHAPTER V.

"YOU must amuse yourself here as best you can till dinner-time, Harry," said his host next morning, as he was mounting his horse. "James will give you the key of the library, and nothing more is wanting to install you in full authority during my absence."

Carleton was not at all averse from being left to himself for some hours in the pensive solitude of the quiet mansion. He had not been able to close his eyes immediately on retiring, fatigued as he was, for thinking of its late occupant, and weaving all manner of imaginary adventures out of the little hank of party-colored material, which Dick's strange narrative had furnished; and when he did fall asleep, the memory of that disjointed story he had been listening to and trying to put together in congruous and intelligible form, still lingered and haunted him in a tantalizing dream, in which he seemed to be chasing a phantom shape through scenes he had read of, until they were as familiar to his imagination as any spot known to his school-boy rambles. Now he saw it toiling painfully up some rugged Alpine steep, and ever and anon resting on its staff and gazing wistfully

6

at the glittering peak, which mocked its daring
aim; then it appeared to be gliding like a shadow
among mouldering ruins and crumbling fanes, or
vanishing in the cloistered gloom of solemn min-
ster or grim sepulchral vault; then, again, it is
seen standing lonely and weird on the deck of the
storm-driven vessel, and straining its wild, yearning eyes over the dark and barren waste of waters,
and, at last, it returns to find its only rest under
the canopy of the loving oak, whose mighty arms
stretch forth and clasp the wanderer in an eternal
embrace.

On awaking from his fevered trance—sleep it
could hardly be called—he found it impossible to
shake off the enchantment of those nightly visions,
and at breakfast his host did not fail to note the
air of musing and absent-minded soberness, which
was so much at variance with his wonted rollick-
some and debonair gaiety. Alloway did not venture
to ask for an explanation of his guest's unusual
pensiveness, for fear of bringing on another fit of
teasing, and, with the ordinary polite commonplaces,
left him to chew the cud of whatever fancy had
taken possession of his thoughts.

After a short stroll over the lawn and through
the garden, Carleton. returned to the house, and
taking the key from the servant, proceeded to the
library. He could not repress a slight feeling of
awe as he turned the key in the lock, but it disappeared as soon as he opened the door.

The sun, streaming in at the windows, bathed
the apartment in a quivering flood of mellow radiance, and far from presenting the gloomy array he

had pictured, every object wore the brightest and
most cheerful aspect. The heavy walls and ceiling
paneled in grained oak, and glistening with a new
coat of varnish; the solid furniture of shining
mahogany and black walnut without speck or stain;
the well-filled book-cases, around which no sign of
cobwebs and venerable dust was clinging—these
certainly were not the common appurtenances of an
anchorite's devotional retreat. In one corner of the
room stood a large, old-fashioned cabinet, or "secretary," profusely embellished with brass ornaments
in the highest state of polish, and opposite to this
was a glass case of imposing dimensions, which
was stored with an *omnium gatherum* of rare curi-
osities—mineral substances in endless variety, relics
of art, *objets-de-vertu*, and the like—a sight such
as would make a virtuoso's heart leap for joy, and
prove by no means uninteresting to the man of
real science. The ample fireplace was adorned with
huge brass andirons, on which the wood was piled
ready to be kindled; a substantial fender of the
same material protected the uncarpeted and wax-pol-
ished floor, and they, the andirons and fender, as
well as the shovel, poker and tongs, were burnished
to a degree of immaculate brilliancy that was marvellous to behold. In the middle of the room was
a large, round table, on which were writing mate-
rials, several books, and bundles of papers neatly
tied up and sealed, and by its side stood an ancient
heirloom in the shape of a capacious easy-chair,
lined with morocco and padded with hair, and having
a contrivance for writing or resting a book attached
to one of its arms. The mantlepiece was decorated

with a pair of massive silver-plated candelabra, two handsome-figured porcelain vases, and various specimens of Wedgewood's ornamental wares, and in a niche above it was a terra-cotta bust, which passed current, on what authority is not stated, for a speaking likeness of the renowned founder of Jamestown colony; one or two bronze statuettes, on brackets, of famous mythological characters, a few select pictures of English hunting and pastoral scenes, a dozen chairs of sundry patterns, a commodious sofa, and an inviting settee, or kind of lounge; these, with the books on the shelves, the map on the wall, the dove-colored window curtains and one large portrait, complete our tame description of this fairer dwelling of heavenly pensive contemplation than the awful monastic cell to which she has been ruthlessly consigned by Pope and Parnell's melancholy muse. The deeply-recessed windows looked out on a wildering maze of shrubs and flowers, whose glories had fled the approach of winter, and at no great distance in the background towered, in regal pomp of purple and gold, the majestic forest, which was Woodbourne's envied ornament and pride. Through the latter a wide and deep ravine, making a natural vista, afforded a tantalizing glimpse of the lovely prospect beyond, bounded by the dark-blue line of the Potomac, and the softer azure-hued "silent hills and more than silent skies" of Maryland. Within, every object was bright and alluring, and without it was so dreamy and still it seemed as if all the world, like the cat demurely dozing on the garden fence, had gone to sleep under the drowsy influence of the delicious November haze—

> Whose vapory folds o'er the landscape strays
> And half involves the woodland maze,
>   Like an early widow's veil,
> Where dimpling tissues from the gaze,
> The form half hides and half betrays,
>   Of beauty wan and pale.

Whatever of agony and torturing care the self-exiled wanderer may have suffered elsewhere, or what the pangs, if any, he endured in secret at home, assuredly they could not be laid to the charge of the tutelary genius of this delightsome abode. Such was Carleton's internal conviction as he took in the whole charming scene at a glance, before pausing to inspect the portrait which confronted him. It was that of a rosy-cheeked, fair-haired boy of sixteen summers, surprisingly beautiful and radiant with the "purple light of love and bloom of young desire." Looking on that exquisite picture, how vividly came rushing into his memory the mournful numbers of that psalm of life he knew by heart, and there was an unsuspected pathos and depth of feeling in his voice as he repeated aloud the lines,

> Yet see how all around them wait,
> The ministers of human fate,
> And black misfortune's baleful train!

Could that handsome cavalier, proud, self-reliant, panoplied in complete armor for the fray in the times which tried men's souls, have had a premonition of the evil days to come? Had the unseen hand of the wizard pushed aside the mystical curtain for a moment, and revealed to his gaze the maimed and broken wreck of a noble form, racked

6*

upon a bed of suffering, on a lonely island, and
dying far from wife, and children, and friends, and
sacred home? He turned away with a sigh, and
walked to the book-case. Having diverted himself
there for awhile with turning over the leaves of
one or two books, and discovered that he was in
no humor for reading, he at last fell to contemplating the old secretary in the corner, and sur-
mising what it might have hid away in its numberless receptacles. There was no telling how old
it was; it had the unmistakable impress of hoar
antiquity; had witnessed, no doubt, the passing
away of several generations, and consequently possessed the irresistible attractions which surround the
proverbial tomb of secrets in every old house. It
should be remarked, however, that we Virginia
people have a queer delusion on the subject of anti-
quarianism, and are in the habit of speaking invariably of the Old Dominion, of colonial memory, in
that venerating way which seems to imply an
antediluvian existence, and of our blessed great
grandams as if they flourished at a period when
"Pharaoh's mother's mother's mummy" was a crispy-
headed marvel of toddling babyhood.

To resume, our young friend was in the best
possible frame of mind to indulge a roving, listless
curiosity, and he felt himself drawn towards the
mysterious object in the corner by an invisible
power. He could not forbear smiling at the eager-
ness with which he found himself approaching it.
How ridiculous, he thought, the idea of expecting
to discover anything here which would throw a ray
of light on the subject of his idle cogitations. Of

course, every hole and cranny had been probed and peered into a hundred times over. Still he could not divest himself of a certain vague, undefined sensation that he was treading on the verge of a wonderful revelation—due in a great measure to the reflection he was then making, that Dick had only examined his uncle's papers in a careless, perfunctory manner, without reference to any particular inquiry, and, therefore, had probably overlooked or forgotten many things which he might consider extremely significant in clearing up the mystery concerning the late Mr. Austin and the Catholic priest. The first drawer he opened contained naught but a pile of uninviting rubbish, newspapers, pamphlets, loose sheets of paper torn from old ledgers, mingled in a confused mass, which showed the little value in which they were held, and the many times they had been rummaged over; so with the second and the third, which, in addition to the trumpery we have mentioned, were filled with an endless assortment of disabled household utensils. The fourth drawer was more attractive in appearance, though it, too, promised very little towards rewarding the painful researches of a curiosity hunter, presenting, as it did, one sea of letters upon letters, some of them tied up in packages, whilst others lying open were fastened together in piles by a thread, as if arranged for easy reference. They bore the address of Mr. John Austin, and embraced the greater portion of his voluminous correspondence with distinguished men of his day, on topics of public interest—matter, perchance, valuable to the future historian of the colony, but wholly uncon-

cerned with the fortunes of the recluse. There was
a MS. among them, which proved to be an unfinished memoir and biographical sketch of his father,
on which Mr. Richard Austin was employed at the
time of his death. Having given this a hurried
perusal, and entertained himself for some time with
skimming over old letters, in which politics, the
price of tobacco and negroes, religious squabbles,
Indian depredations, Braddock's expedition, and other
matters relating to the welfare of the colony before
he was born, were mixed in an inextricable mélange,
Carleton was about to close the drawer, when a
familiar hand-writing on the back of one of the
bundles of letters he had not disturbed arrested his
attention. It was from his father, who had once
been Mr. John Austin's colleague in the House of
Burgesses. He untied the package, and examined
the contents. The letters were all from the same
source, and of the same general purport—consulting and comparing opinions on legislative matters.
All but one, which appeared to be strangely out
of place in that company, intruded there evidently
through inadvertence. These documents had been
carefully inspected by the author of the MS., as
was shown by the copious extracts of them he had
made. The interloping epistle was addressed to
Richard Austin, Esquire, Gent.; N—— Store,
W—— County, Virginia. As Carleton stood holding
the letter in his hand, and looking wonderingly at
the strange superscription, he again felt the sensation of mysterious awe creeping over him.

"Psha!" said he, striving to throw off the spell
with a contemptuous shrug; "what childish folly is

this! One would think I was in the very act of
unrolling the dread scroll of fate, and reading what
it had in store for me, when, in fact, I am only
halloing my idle fancy on a wild-goose chase. There
is nothing in Mr. Richard Austin's melancholy history can affect my career in life. Yet, how do I
know that? Who can foretell the influence which
one man's lightest act or word may have on the
fortunes of others? Is not each of us a link in
the chain of inscrutable destiny? But a truce to
moralizing; let's see what is here." He opened the
letter, and read as follows:

LONDON, Feb. 12, o.s., 1775.

MY DEAR SIR:

Yours, under date of November 16th, 1774, came to
hand only a fortnight ago, the vessel having been delayed
on the voyage over by stress of weather. Agreeable to
your wishes, I lost no time in calling upon Sir William
Markham, M.P., at his lodgings in this city. Our interview was of the most pleasant and satisfactory character. Waiving preliminaries, I showed him your letter,
remarking that it would best explain the nature of my
business. He perused it with grave interest, and, as
I thought, suppressed emotion. After which he said,
"Please do me the kindness to say to Mr. Austin, that I
duly received his communication, and that my failure to
acknowledge it involves a tedious and painful explanation, which shall be made as soon as I can command
sufficient leisure." He then told me of a visit he had
from a Catholic priest, who was apparently interested
about the same subject, and whom he had treated very
cavalierly, to say the least, not having deigned even to
ask his name. Was that person in Mr. Austin's confidence? If so, where could he be found? I replied that
I had never heard you speak of such a person in con-

nection with him, and that I would advise you of the circumstance in my answer to your letter. With that our conference ended.

The master of the *Speedwell* has just called to inform me that his vessel will drop down on the next tide, and to know if I wish to send anything on board. As I have several little commissions to dispatch, I must bring this letter to a close. Please tell Mr. Copland that his matter received prompt attention; I sent remittance to him last week in exchange on Amsterdam, for fear of accidents. I yet hope and believe we will arrive at a good understanding with the colonies. Let me hear from you by the first opportunity. Communication with America is becoming more and more uncertain every day. Did you get the books shipped per packet *Rover?* I am pleased to hear that your health continues to improve. With best wishes, I remain,

Faithfully, your friend and obedient servant,

JAMES BUCHANAN.

"February 12th, 1775," repeated Carleton, looking back at the date of the letter; "received April 6th, and answered on the 15th of the same month. Mr. Austin died shortly after; and so ends the chapter. How provoking. It is plain that Dick has not seen this letter. The priest again. Can he be the same Julian Soulé? I have a mind to write to Mr. Carroll." The sound of hurried footsteps in the hall interrupted the train of his thoughts, and he barely had time to thrust the letter in his bosom before Alloway came bursting into the room.

"Halloo, old fellow," he exclaimed, in his hearty way, as his eye fell on the open drawer of the secretary; "what the deuce are you up to there? Could you find nothing better to console you for

my absence than is to be got by gnawing at the
mouldy bare bones in that lumber chest? Come,
I am sure you need something to wash your throat
and help your digestion after such a musty repast.
You see I am back sooner than I promised," he
rattled on, while Carleton was re-arranging the contents of the drawer. "One of the referees was sick,
and the case had to be laid over. I would have
been here an hour ago, if I had not chanced to
fall in with Bob Temple on the road. He is always
brimful of news, and is a kind of good-natured,
gossiping burr that one finds hard to shake off.
To tell the truth, I relish a little of Bob once in
a while, taken fresh, but he gets to be consumedly
boring on too long and too frequent acquaintance.
Still, there is no great harm in the prattling jay-
bird of a creature. He had been to Clifton, he
said, to pay his respects to the foreign gentleman
from France, who is Colonel Littleton's guest. 'Foreign gentleman,' said I; 'do you mean the fellow
who bolted into our chase yesterday, and out again,
like a clap of thunder?' 'The very same,' replied
Bob. 'You see, one of the colonel's *hands* was down
at my house betimes this morning for a load of
oysters, and he told me as how his master and
young mistress were just, the day before yesterday,
come home from Maryland, and brought with them
a mighty nice gentleman, they called Mr. Conrad—a
beau Miss Mary had caught somewhere over the
river. So I thought it was the civil thing to do
for me to ride up and call on the distinguished
stranger, for between us, not to go any farther,
there is no manner of doubt about it, he is a count

or marquis, or something of the sort, as sure as a
gun's iron.' 'Marquis, fiddlesticks!' said I; 'more
likely a runagate of a dancing master, or abscond-
ing *valèt-de-chambre*. Did you see him?' 'No,' said
he, 'he was gone to ride with Miss Littleton. I
sat some time waiting for them to return, when
who should walk in but my especial aversion, old
Jake Thompson'—he gave Bob his title of Daily
Postman—'he was come for his usual dish of politics with the colonel, and they were soon at it
tooth and nail, talking, and swearing, and gesticu-
lating like mad. That sort of fuming and raving
did not suit me, so I left my compliments for the
marquis, and promised to call again.' Marquis,
quotha! and this philandering Monsieur Magnifico
is Miss Littleton's latest conquest. A second Portia
is my fair cousin, and this another Colchos strand
for many Jasons," and Dick closed the library
door with a bang, and led the way to the dining-
room in the loftiest imaginable state of scornful
incredulity. Carleton was too busily occupied with
his own thoughts to pay attention to this disdainful
ebullition. When they had finished their toddy, and
were seated together on the porch, he adroitly turned
the conversation into the channel in which he
wished it to flow.

CHAPTER VI.

IT had not escaped his guest's keen observation that Mr. Richard Alloway was more deeply agitated than he cared to acknowledge by that incident concerning the Catholic priest. Evidently, it had not before occurred to him that there was aught. of especial interest in his uncle's lonely career to anybody but his own family and small circle of friends. His emotion, on hearing Carleton's story, was that of undisguised wonder at a most unexpected revelation. The fact that a stranger, whose name he did not remember to have ever heard from Mr. Austin's lips, was so much interested to find him out, was well calculated to excite in a less sensitive mind than Dick's something more serious than a transitory feeling of curiosity. Duly respecting the tender and affectionate reverence with which his friend invested the memory of his uncle, Carleton observed the utmost delicacy in approaching the subject.

"What a charming library you have, Dick," said he; "nothing of the awful or mysterious to be seen there."

"It is the brightest spot about the house," replied Dick; "everything is just as uncle left it, except

7   (73)

the portrait, which took the place of one of my grandfather I pointed out to you in the hall. He had the room repaired and newly painted last spring shortly before his death. He was very partial to it, and spent a third of his time there in the old arm-chair beside the table."

Harry.—"How did he occupy himself?"

Dick.—"Usually, in reading and meditation; latterly he wrote a good deal, being interested in preparing memoirs of his father and other eminent men of that day. You may have seen the MS. among those old papers?"

Harry.—"I read portions of it; he has paid my father the compliment of quoting extensively from his letters to Mr. John Austin. He was alone, I imagine, the greater part of the time."

Dick.—"Yes; frequently during the day and always at night until his regular hour for retiring, he had the room entirely to himself. It was his custom of a morning and evening, when the weather was good, to walk awhile in the garden and look after the flowers, of which he was very fond, and now and then he would have his chair brought out in the shade of the oak tree on the lawn; still, with Prospero, he might truthfully say, his library was his dukedom."

Harry.—"And you are positively certain he left nothing in the way of writings except the unfinished memoirs?"

Dick.—"That is certainly my firm belief."

Harry.—"You have, then, made a thorough search among his papers?"

Dick.—"His papers? Why he left nothing but

what you saw. Most of that rubbish in the old
secretary was a legacy from my grandfather; I have
never had the least inclination, to say nothing of the
leisure, to overhaul it. As for the unfinished memoirs, *pendunt opera interrupta*, and so they are likely
to remain for this generation, if they look to me
for completion. But why are you so inquisitive,
Harry? did you find a mare's nest in that ancient
heirloom? By Jove! old fellow—" It should be
remarked in this place, *par parenthese*, that Mr.
Richard Alloway had a habit of frequently appeal-
ing, in a familiar manner, to the great Olympian
Thunderer, whether as a meaningless expletive
merely, or a convenient rhetorical safety-valve, or as
his peculiar way of making known his veneration
of the ancient classics, we cannot undertake to say.
"By Jove! old fellow, I verily believe you are a
regular professor of black magic. That look, now,
'angels and ministers of grace defend us!' Do
they teach necromancy in your famous Wittenberg
in New Jersey?"

Carleton laughed, and putting off the mask of
simulated awe he had waggishly assumed, "Don't
be alarmed, Dick," said he; "I am not trying to
work upon your superstitious fears. My questioning
was only intended to make certain whether you
had ever seen this letter."

Alloway took it from his hand, and seeing to
whom it was addressed, became, on an instant, very
grave and thoughtful. When he had perused it
twice over, he fell into a profound reverie, and
began whistling in a low undertone—a sign, as his
friend well knew, that he was perplexed to an

extraordinary degree. Carleton, too, dropped into a
brown study. To his susceptible imagination, the
· letter revealed a fascinating scene of wild and
startling conjecture. It was like a voice from the
grave of the buried past, whose weird, unearthly
tone vibrated on his heart, and called up a throng
of fantastic and shadowy images. The torturing illu-
sions of his last night's dream faded into nothing-
ness before the consciousness of some unknown life·
mystery which lay hidden, as he conceived, under
the ivy green an arrow's flight from where he sat,
pondering on the strange words he had read.

"You observed the allusion there to the priest,
Dick," he at length said, musingly; "he is the
veritable *deus ex machina* of our mystery. Of course
it can be no other than the Abbé Julian Soulé."

"Like enough," replied Dick; "but it was not of
him I was thinking. Markham, Markham—why,
that was the name of the unfortunate hero of
uncle's pathetic little romance; and, what is like-
wise remarkable, the other prominent character, a
lady, was called Conrad; it is an Italian story of
cruelty and revenge."

Harry.—"Do tell it to me, Dick."

Dick.—"No, no; I would not like to mar it by
a hap-hazard recital; besides, it is too long to
remember. I have it written down in my commonplace book just as uncle narrated it, and another time
you may read it for yourself. Let me see; where
was it that I saw mention of Sir William Markham?
Oh, I remember now; in looking over a batch of
old English newspapers on the top of one of those
book-cases in the library. It occurs in an account

of the proceedings in Parliament; he is reported to have made a strong speech in defence of the people of Massachusetts. The passage was marked with a pencil, but I did not see anything specially noteworthy in it."

Harry.—"And nothing further has been heard from Mr. Buchanan?"

Dick.—"O, yes; I have had one letter from uncle's factor; I'll show it to you, it is such a perfect model of commercial neatness and brevity." He went in, and soon came back with an open letter, which he handed Carleton, who read it as follows:

CHEAPSIDE, LONDON, 12th Aug., 1775.

ESTEEMED SIR:

Inclosed please find account of my late correspondent, Mr. Richard Austin (whose sole devisee and legatee I am advised you are), stated to date of his demise, showing balance to his credit of £967, 8s. 6½d., which is subject to your instructions.

Begging you to accept the assurance of my sincere condolence in your recent sad bereavement, I subscribe myself,

Most respectfully, your obedient humble servant,

JAMES BUCHANAN, Merchant.

For MR. RICH'D A. ALLOWAY.

"Neat as a copper plate, and, doubtless, very correct; but not a syllable about the baronet and the priest," said Carleton.

"And pray," said Dick, "why should Mr. Buchanan suppose that I felt any interest in these distinguished persons?"

Harry.—"Nothing was more reasonable than for

7*

him to infer that Mr. Richard Austin's favorite
nephew shared his intimate confidence, and ought,
therefore, to be informed of whatever pertained to his
private and peculiar transactions."

Dick.—"Then, I am glad he did not take your
very reasonable view of the case. It is my opinion
that there is nothing to be gained by boggling after
this plaguey will-o'-wisp of a mystery, as you call
it, which, if found out, would be of as little concern
to you and me as what is this moment coming to
pass at the Antipodes," with which conclusive
remark, Alloway folded up the merchant's letters
and put them in his pocket.

Carleton was not a little puzzled by his friend's
nonchalance. He could not exactly divine what
was the nature of the sensations which had been
awakened in the young planter's mind by the dis-
closures he had made. Was it real or feigned, his
repugnance to pursuing the investigation? Yet, his
behavior was in keeping with his general character.
His nature was too earnest and matter-of-fact; his
temper too hopeful and elastic to suffer him to
brood over the past, or vex his soul with chasing
the fleeting phantom of a heated imagination. He
was never at a loss for active, wholesome employment for mind and body, and his "bosom's lord
sat lightly on its throne," now that he was assured
by the sacredest of human vows of the joy which is
immeasurably above and beyond all other earthly ben-
isons, the immediate jewel of the soul, requited love.

"It is a tough case," such was Carleton's internal reflection; "but I am not yet disposed to give
it up. I was always expert in unravelling tangled
skeins, and see if I don't yet succeed in running

this thread off on a reel. The first thing to do is to ascertain what the Abbé wants with Mr. Richard Metcalf, otherwise, Austin. That my father can do when he replies to Mr. Carroll's letter. But it occurs to me that Monsieur Conrad may be able to give us some information on the subject; at least, he can tell us who the Abbé is. He came hither from Maryland in Miss Littleton's train, and her sister is a near neighbor to the Carrolls', where the priest is sojourning. Being fellow-countrymen and strangers in a strange land, they must be known to each other. Dick," said he, suddenly arousing his friend from the pleasant doze into which he had fallen, "suppose we call upon the Frenchman in the morning?"

"You must excuse me, Harry," said Dick hastily; "to-morrow I shall be busy at home; besides, I want you to ride with me over the farm. I flatter myself that I have made sundry improvements of late, the hint of which I got from my neighbor, Mr. Graeme. Speaking of him, I am reminded that I have a note of invitation for you to a party at Bonhill; here it is."

"A party?" exclaimed Carleton; "that is lucky. I shall have a chance to see all my friends in a lump. 'Mr. and Mrs. John Graeme will be pleased to see Mr. Carleton at Bonhill on Friday night, instant, on the occasion of their daughter's birthday party.' What a beautiful hand—good sign, says my Lord Chesterfield, of a graceful person and an amiable disposition. Come, old boy, wake up, and tell me all about the Graemes.'

But we will save Mr. Alloway the trouble of complying with that modest request.

CHAPTER VII.

APPILY blended in mutual love and esteem had been the lives of John and Ellen Graeme from the day they plighted troth to each other under the rowan-tree, on the banks of Leven Water, to the date of the present memoirs. Goldenly bright had the hours flown over their heads; their house was the garner of the choicest gifts of fortune, and the neighbors, one and all, came to regard them as an example of matrimonial felicity, which the most inveterate celibate must envy and applaud.

But now again the heavens are hung with black, and the future looks dark and ominous of approaching ills. True, the entire country is involved in a common trouble, the same perils menace all alike; but none of her neighbors had with her experienced the actual calamities of civil war, and the prospect of another sanguinary struggle between 'kinsmen and former friends calls up, with all the dread accompaniments of horror and alarm, the woeful tragedy in which she had borne more than her equal portion of sorrow and suffering. To others it is as yet the vague apprehension of unknown and indefinable ills; to her it is the present reali-

zation of the acme of human misery, the sum of all
the wretchedness that the worst passions of the vilest
men can invoke upon their sinful race; ever the
self-same demon of wrath and desolation, red with
the stains of all the righteous blood shed upon the
earth, whether welling slow, drop by drop, from the
breast of the first victim of murderous rage, or
poured forth in crimson torrents—

When merciless ambition or mad zeal
Has led two hosts of dupes to battlefield,
That, blind, they there may dig each others graves,
And call the sad work, Glory!

Husband and wife had kept, with religious fidelity,
the vow they had made to each other long years
ago, and never a word had passed the lips of either
on the one forbidden topic. But Mr. Graeme cannot help perceiving the change which has come
over his wife's spirits, and he intuitively divines
the secret cause of her trouble. He sees that a
great dread is constantly hanging over her, threat-
ening to fall with crushing weight. Again busy
memory is at work, reviving the agonies which are
past, and filling her soul with wretched forebodings
of worst to come; again—

The field of the slain rushes red on her sight,
And the clans of Culloden are scattered in flight!

Every day she grew more and more nervous and
disquieted, and her husband's anxiety increased in
proportion. Yet she firmly held by their mutual
pledge, and he was waiting for her to release him.
So it went on, until one night Mr. Graeme was
greatly startled to hear her sobbing violently in

her sleep, and repeating, in piteous accents, the
names of her father, brother and son. Next morning the seal of the covenant was broken. She
unbosomed her soul to her husband, and earnestly
besought him to send George away to Scotland
until they saw how these unhappy troubles were
likely to end. The request was an agreeable surprise to the worthy gentleman. He had a project
in reference to his son's future career in life, which
he had forborne to mention since the lad's return
from Williamsburg some months agone, for fear it
would not meet his mother's approval in the then
agitated state of her mind, as it required for its
accomplishment a separation from George of several
years.

Although Mr. John Graeme was never heard to
set up a pretence of being a very profound scholar,
he was by no means so unlearned as to be an
object of pity on a rainy day. In all the branches
of practical and useful information, he was far in
advance of the most polished and polite of his neighbors. It had been his particular pride to keep
abreast with the scientific improvements of the age;
he was familiarly acquainted with the latest inven-
tions of mechanical skill, and had been instru-
mental in introducing some of them to the community in which he resided. When he abandoned mercantile pursuits, he transferred to his new avocation
of farming his entire stock of method, energy and
sagacity, and his example had imparted a fresh
impulse to agricultural development, which was
especially evidenced in the inroads which the culti-
vation of the cereals was beginning to make on

the growth of the great commercial staple of the colony. He was a noble instance of genuine, sturdy independence. He bought nothing abroad which could be as well made at home. No appliances were wanting in his administration to make the business of farming at once easy, economical and remunerative. He had constructed, on his plantation, a smithy and a /large shop, where carpenter, wheelright and cooper's work was done, and where many of the implements and utensils of husbandry were made out and out from the most approved models. Then there was the "ship-yard," at which all manner of small boats and larger river craft were built and repaired; but the splendid "double mills," in the ownership of which his neighbor, Colonel Littleton, claimed a. half interest, were the pride and delight of the whole countryside, turning out flour which rivalled in quality the famous *Mount Vernon* brand, with its unimpeachable inscription, "G. Washington!" The paraphernalia of his peculiar sanctum, the room in which he entertained his particular cronies, displayed the ruling characteristics of his mind; every article of furniture having been manufactured on the spot, from the plentiful supply of material · of maple, oak, cherry, walnut and pine, stored up in the commodious warehouse of the neighboring forest. In short, albeit Mr. John Graeme was theoretically an avowed advocate of free trade and sailors' rights in the broadest sense, he was in practice as perfect an illustration of home-brewed, home-loving, and home-protecting industry and frugality as one rarely meets with now-a-days.

George's fortune was already made, as far as worldly goods were concerned; he should, so his father thought, learn to devote his leisure and means to the prosecution of such useful aims and purposes as here found abundant scope for active exemplification. As a preparation for this field of usefulness, it was designed that the young gentleman should perfect his theoretical studies in physical science at the University of Glasgow, after which he was to visit and inspect its more recent discoveries, as exhibited in the various factories and workshops of Europe.

But whilst Mr. Graeme was no doubt mainly solicitous to see his son embarked on his magnificent voyage of scientific exploration, there was another motive, we have good reason to suspect, for his acceding so promptly to his wife's request. Master George was a remarkably susceptible youth, as the phrase is, and, more is the pity, had fallen madly in love with a lady who did not see fit to return his inordinate attachment. The consequence was, that he had grown, of late, very miserable and melancholy, and his father reasonably concluded that the best remedy for the disease of unrequited love was to be found in "change o' fowk and change o' scene." Secretly, the old gentleman, was himself considerably cut up by his son's lamentable misadventure in the mart of matrimonial speculation. He was an extravagant admirer of Miss Mary Littleton, and had George's suit prospered, he would have hailed the event with beaming satisfaction. As it was, he did not altogether despair of its being a match one of these days. George was

hardly better than a grown-up boy; his education
for the stern pursuits of life was just begun, and
nobody could foresee the difference which a few
years might make in those qualities which attract
a woman's wayward fancy. While the fair maid of
Clifton remained mistress of her inclinations, there
was ground for the hope that she might be per-
suaded to look at the proposition in a more favorable light. So argued *paterfamilias* on the general
theory of probabilities. But we shall presently see
that the capricious divinity, who regulates these little
matters, had decreed that his sanguine calculations
should be cruelly disappointed.

For the reasons we have detailed, Mr. Graeme
consented with alacrity to his wife's entreaties, and
George sailed in the next outward-bound vessel for
Glasgow. There let us leave him for the present, to
quench the flame of his ill-starred passion, and at
the same time to temper the ardor of his patriotic
soul by contact with the discreet and calculating
burghers of that aspiring and eminently loyal metropolis. When he was gone, and had written to
tell them of his safe arrival in Scotland, and of
the pleasant reception he had met with among his
father's friends and relatives there, his mother
appeared to be greatly relieved, regained much of
her old cheerfulness, and went about her household duties with the diligence and grace which
were the ruling traits of her disposition. Thus desperately she clung to the faint hope of a happy
issue out of this last great affliction, and watched
with wistful eyes and palpitating heart every sign
and portent of the political heavens. But the clouds

8

continued to gather thick and fast, and every day the palpable darkness was increasing; now the air was filled with the sulphury vapor of war; the Revolution was begun in earnest, and Mrs. Graeme's faith in the emblematical evening sky was shaken as a reed. The hour was fast approaching; she felt it was close at hand when the irrevocable decision must be made, and while she prayed the more fervently that she might yet be spared the dreadful ordeal, her heart indignantly spurned the base suggestion that her darling son would prove a recreant to the cause of his native land. Now that she saw the fearful alternative could not be much longer avoided, she sought to divert her mind from the contemplation of the painful scene by constant employment. In vain her husband protested that she was over-exerting herself; she only smiled at his remonstrances, and said he was mistaken; the work was good for her. Thus she continued to pay the most assiduous attention to every demand of duty until an untoward accident compelled her desist.

There had been a sort of epidemic prevailing in the neighborhood during the month of August of this year—a virulent type of fever—of which the medical faculty were at loss for an explanation. The distemper was said to be contagious, and every precaution was taken to prevent its spreading. Bonhill did not escape its ravages; half of the servants were taken down with it, and the other half were stupefied with terror, waiting for their time to come. Amid this scene of suffering and dismay there moved a ministering spirit with the balm of solacing joy and healing on its wings. It was the lovely mis-

tress of the manor, fulfilling her mission with that
serene, unshrinking heroism, which shames the highest courage of man. The plague abated, and, thanks
to her unwearied exertions, there was not a single
death from its effects on the plantation.

By a miracle of mercy the good matron escaped
its fangs, but the fatigue and exposure she had
undergone in nursing the sick so impaired her
health and weakened her constitution, that her physician peremptorily commanded her to refrain from
her accustomed labors. Thus, reluctantly constrained,
she sought the needful refreshment of rest, and surrendered the sceptre for a time into her daughter's
hand. And, her father's word for it, that young
lady wielded it in queenly style.

Where is the woman that does not exult to exercise authority,—in her rightful sphere, of course?
It was amusing to see the old gentleman, who was
used to nothing short of unquestioned obedience,
watching the little woman as she bustled about the
house, issuing her commands, and showing her love
of sway in a thousand nameless ways. Especially
did he note the delight it gave her to move all the
portable property in that inner shrine of his at least
once a day without the slightest provocation, merely
to intimate that her will was the supreme law of
the establishment. He offered not a word of remonstrance or complaint against such outrageous display
of arbitrary power; indeed he rather encouraged her
to play the imperial role on the grandest scale.
The day would come when she would have a little
domestic kingdom of her own, and it was high·time
she was learning how to govern it. Like other vice-

royal personages, she was frequently a trifle more
exacting and unnecessarily fussy than there was any
occasion for; and she never failed to resent the
least hint that she was in any wise departing from
the established rules of the legitimate sovereign.
"Ole Missis didn't do dat way" was an affront not
to be tolerated, even from Aunt Dinah, a venerable
domestic oracle whom her mother often deigned to
consult. Miss Lucy was not content with sporting
the tawdry trappings of place; her maxim was,
Aut Cæsar, aut nullus; she would be the real
fountain of dignity and power, or else not wear the
purple robe at all. Errors and blunders she might
commit at first; but better these than irresolution,
weakness and vacillation. First establish your throne
was what she said to herself; impress your subjects
with becoming deference and respect of your authority; learn to command; the minor details of
administration are easily learned by observation and
practice. This was her code, and, to our thinking,
Machievilli nor Oxensteirn could have expressed it
with more sententious and discerning perspicacity.

The neighbors were wont to say of Lucy that
she was her father's own dear child. In certain
prominent traits of character, as well as in personal
appearance, there was a striking likeness between
father and daughter. The same sunshiny and mirth-
ful disposition; the same self-reliance and firmness,
blended with gentleness and forbearance towards
others; the same large-hearted and spontaneous be-
nevolence; the same shrewd and penetrating common
sense and even placidity of temper; the same in-
stinctive abhorrence of ill-natured carping and evil-

speaking—in a word, every quality for which the one was noted found its counterpart in the other. If not the bonniest, she was the most irresistibly charming and winsome of lassies. Her figure was slight, though far from being fragile, and her every movement was the perfection of unconstrained grace. Her complexion was a rich combination of unrivalled tints; her temples were literally crowned with a golden diadem of sunny locks; her eyes, the color of the cloudless sky, beamed with playful mirth and mischief, and her smile was a foretaste of the joys of heaven. She had her mother's rare gift of music, and her voice was melody itself. True, the harpsichord was the only instrument she had ever learned to play on, and singing simple ballads and hymns was the extent of her vocal attainments, but in these her execution was unrivalled, and she was justly regarded as a musical prodigy in all the region around and about.

Her sweetest songs were those of her father's native land. She had the whole of Allan Ramsay's collection by heart, and she learned them not merely for the sake of gratifying Mr. Graeme's clannish devotion to the customs and associations of Scotland, but because there was an indescribable charm to her in the language itself, which rendered it so far superior to her mother tongue in expressing the tenderest and most exquisite touches of sentiment, humor and pathos. In this way, too, she acquired so great familiarity with the dialect and current literature of Scotland, that between her mother and herself, her father was never at a loss for a pleasant companion in his rambles whenever he felt inclined,

8*

as he often did, "to gae daunering like a ghaist
amang the sweet and mournfu' memories o' lang
syne."

And when the morning and evening air was
vocal with her delicious warblings, he was never
heard to lament that there were no linties in the
Bonhill woods. Thus joyous and loving, tender and
true, surrounded by all holy influences, enshrined
in her happy home like a pearl in its shell, grew
into the perfect form of modest maidenhood, this
"so fair a thing, so free from mortal taint."

To-morrow come and gone, Miss Lucy Graeme
will have reached her eighteenth birthday. The joyful event is to be celebrated with appropriate fes-
tivities—with music, dancing and feasting, amid the
happy congratulations of her numerous young friends
and admirers. The invitations have gone out through
the length and breadth of the neighborhood, and
there is sure to be a goodly gathering of the beauty
and chivalry of the Old Dominion under Mr.
Graeme's hospitable roof-tree. In those days a wed-
ding was the especial grand occasion for the display of cheerful hilarity and festive munificence;
but then, as now, and as it ever will and ought
to be, young folks would be young folks, and they
were not slow in finding or inventing pretexts for
frolic, fun and glee, as outlets and safety-valves for
the effervescing spirits of abounding gaiety and
light-hearted mirth.

CHAPTER VIII.

THE friends have returned from their visit to Bonhill. A fire has been kindled in the library, and there we now find them. The visitor is reclining negligently on the sofa, loosely arrayed in dressing gown and slippers, garterless stockings and open shirt collar, and enjoying, to the utmost degree, the luxurious ease without troubling his head about the dignity of the position. He looks dreamily up at the ceiling, and runs his fingers through his hair in a ruminating way. In striking contrast to this picture of musing indolence, mine host is sitting bolt-upright in a straight-back chair, with a resigned and martyr-like aspect, presenting a complacent exhibition of the loftiest qualities of heroism and fortitude under the most trying circumstances. He is gazing fixedly at the rugged bust over the mantle-piece, and is obviously rehearsing in imagination the part of the redoubtable warrior in the famous scene where the murderous club is hovering over his devoted head, and he, wholly in the dark concerning the humane intentions of the lovely Pocahontas, swears a soldierly prayer or two preparatory to taking final leave of his senses.

Carleton (loquiter).—"Dick," said he, "I am delighted with your Scotch neighbor; was never more agreeably entertained than I have been this evening, saving your delectable company."

"Ah, indeed," was the reply; "I am heartily glad you were so much pleased with your visit. It is a pity, though, we did not stay to supper. Such ambrosial porridge, such nectareous usquebagh, and, O *Apicius!* what a hantle o' gude eating there is about a swine!"

Harry.—"Don't be a fool, Dick. I hope you have not repeated that contemptible saying of Dr. Johnson at my expense. The joke would have been sorry enough in the mouth of a clown; coming from a grave moralist, it was simply disgusting."

Dick (paying no regard to the energetic disclaimer).—"I say, Harry, what a deal of humor there is in those lines of Churchill. You remember? The "Prophecy of Famine."

> Two boys whose birth, beyond all question, springs
> From great and glorious, though forgotten kings,
> Shepherds of Scottish lineage—

I forget the rest, but it was intensely witty and droll—the part about Sawny and Jockey, and the Highland lass who scratched her lover into rest and sank pleased and hungry on his breast."

Harry.—"Stuff and nonsense. Churchill was a coarse, vulgar calumniator—just what Hogarth painted him—a beer-drinking bear in a dirty, black gown."

Dick (still impassably severe of mein).—"Of course you undertook to enlighten the benighted Jockey

on politics and got a taunt of one that makes
better fritters of English than Parson Hugh in the
play, 'Hout, tout, lad; dinna fash yer noddle wi'
sic and orra deal o' fusionless whigmaleries, it's
fient a bit else but an auld toot on a new horn,
yer screed o' independence and a' that. What ken
ye noo o' the steam engine?'"

"Admirably mimicked, Dick," cried Carleton, clap-
ping his hands with delight and laughing heartily.
"What a genius you have for the languages. But
amor vincit omnia, to win the daughter you would
learn to gabble all the barbarous dialects that were
ever grunted or squeaked since the building of
Babel. Is Miss Lucy like her father?"

"The young lady," replied the imperturable Richard, who all this while had not taken his eyes
from the effigy of the Jamestown hero, "is reputed
to possess the combined excellent qualities of both
her parents. In personal appearance, she is strikingly like her father."

Harry.—"Then, sir, I give you fair warning; look
to your girth and stirrups, I am coming at you
full tilt."

"I accept the gage, most peerless mirror of knighthood," retorted Dick, "and will contest the prize
in accordance with the ancient laws and usages of
our illustrious and never-to-be too highly extolled
order."

"Gallantly spoken, renowned Cid, Amadis de Gaul,
Guy of Warwick, or—"

"Captain John Smith," exclaimed Dick, with
emphatic gusto; "he is my *beau-ideal* of chivalry;
worth an army of your huge iron-clad, spine-cleavers

of romance. Where would we be now if it had
not been for him?"

Harry.—"A shrewd question, truly, Sir Knight;
in my opinion, we might have been in a much
worse place. But as Horatio says in the play, that
were to inquire too curiously. I agree with you; the
Smiths are an ancient, honorable and powerful clan,
and our John Smith, of glorious memory, was the
greatest son of Vulcan that ever forged a horse-
shoe or a · thunderbolt. If he had only · rounded
the period by marrying the dusky maiden he would
have been the bright, particular star of chivalry,
totus, teresatque rotundus! By the beard of the
immortal Cid Hamete Ben Engeli, he should have
married her had she been a common scullery wench,
and her complexion the 'shadowed livery of the
burnished sun,' instead of being what she really
was—a royal model of innocent simplicity and untutored loveliness,—copper-colored, to be sure, *sed ne
nimium crede colori!* Honor bright, don't you consider that to be a black spot on the otherwise
untarnished escutcheon of the paragon of Smiths?"

Dick.—"I don't view it in that light. Suppose
he did not love the girl?"

Harry.—"Answered like the silly, sighing Strephon
you are. What had love to do with it, simpleton?
It was a question of sheer gratitude; and, more
Latin for you, the poet tells us, *ingratum si dixa-
eris, omnia dices!* It was most reprehensible conduct in Captain John Smith, say what you please;
and history will set a cross mark against it in
spite of the brilliant renown of his warlike deeds."

Dick.—"He wasn't near so much to blame as

was the pious founder of the Roman colony in his treatment of Madam Dido; and isn't he cracked up by Virgil and the rest as a marvellous proper man ?"

Harry.—"It is not a parallel case, my boy, by any means. Æneas' work had been allotted him by inexorable fate, and espousing the pretty Dido was not included in the programme. He was like Ulysses dallying at the Calypso isle while Ithaca was yet afar. With Captain John Smith it was entirely different. There was nothing to prevent his taking a wife at the time; and to my mind, there was poetic fitness in his offering his hand to the generous woman who had saved his life, and who, laying aside the prejudice of caste, was worthy to mate with a hero; but he did not do it, and the romance was sadly marred."

Dick.—"For that matter, there was ever so thrilling a tragedy spoiled on that memorable occasion. If, as you surmise, this lovely Ariadne of the western wilds was so frantically enamored of our hero, why in the name of Melpomene did she not jump in the river and drown herself, when she saw it was a hopeless case?"

The sprightly cavalier was nonplussed by this unexpected turn of the subject.

"I cry quits, Dick," said he. "And now, sir, explain, where were your manners that you did not introduce me to the Bonhill beauty this evening?"

"That's the crow you have to pick with me, is it?" replied Dick. "A pretty question, indeed. I might as well ask, where was your gallantry that you did not pay due homage to the lady in question? You told me your business with Mr. Graeme would not take up a minute's time, and there you were closeted together, like a couple of sage privy councillors, for two mortal hours. After the interview, you sent me word that you were ready to go, and I obeyed your wishes. You did not once mention the lady's name."

Harry.—"All right, old fellow; the fact is, I preferred making my first bow *en grand tenue* to-morrow night, and as I found Mr. Graeme to be most excellent company—" ("And his wine did not smack of creosote," interjected Dick.) "And you were not at all averse from having Miss Lucy all to yourself in the garden, there is—"

Dick.—"Nothing more to be said on the subject."

Harry.—"No—yes, Dick; about this Frenchman, now, I am consumedly puzzled—"

Dick.—"So am I."

Harry.—"How so?"

Dick.—"Just to know what the pesky, outlandish jack-a-dandy is to you, that you should be taking so much trouble on yourself about him and his affairs."

Harry.—"Exactly what your good Scotch neighbor remarked, booby, only he was not so emphatically polite in his manner of putting the question."

Dick.—"Mr. Graeme? what the deuce does he know about the Frenchman?"

Harry.—"Nothing, further than that he is the guest of Col. Littleton, who picked him up in Maryland when he went to fetch his daughter home. Still, there was no call that I could see for the remark he made—that he did not deem it incum-

bent on him to be 'speering after ilka sorner in
the hale country side.' The topic was evidently
distasteful, and he dismissed it with little ceremony.
What possible grudge can he have against this Mr.
Conrad?"

Dick.—"Mr. Graeme is the last man in the world
to form unfavorable opinions of people without just
cause. I'll be bound he has a good reason for his
apparent incivility."

Harry.—"There's the rub—that same 'good reason'; but now I think of it, let's have that little
romance you spoke of; I'm just in the mood for
listening."

Dick.—"The mischief you are; well, anything to
keep your everlasting tongue quiet for a brief space."

So saying, he went to the table, and unlocking
a drawer, produced a folio as large as a merchant's
ledger; then having drawn the table nearer the
fire, placed on it the light from the mantlepiece,
and opened the book at the proper page.

"There, voracious quidnunc," said he, "the feast
is prepared; come and satisfy your curious soul."

"Thanks, my very kind host," retorted Carleton;
"I much prefer getting satisfaction through the
medium of my ears, first and foremost, because I
am not inclined to change my pleasant berth; and,
secondly, and chiefly, because it would take away
the relish from the repast for me to have to spell
my way through such 'a d—d cramped piece of
penmanship,' so take your seat and begin, there's
a good boy."

"A plague on his impudence," muttered Alloway,
mechanically dropping into the chair. "Call that a

9

bad hand; why, I can read it like a book." With
which boastful assertion, he snuffed the candles,
cleared his throat, and launched *ore rotundo* into
"My uncle's story."

CHAPTER IX.

IN the Autumn of 17—," said uncle, "I set out from Geneva, where I was sojourning, for a ramble on foot through the northern provinces of Italy. Traveling at leisure, I took no definite route, but wandered from place to place as momentary fancy or inclination dictated. In this way, I found myself in the midst of a wild and picturesque region among the mountains of Tyrol. Loitering incautiously to view the numberless sights of natural interest which met my gaze at every step, darkness overtook me some miles from the ancient city of Meran, where I expected to spend the night. I was on the top of a mountain, the road was rugged and dangerous, and to make the situation worse, an ugly storm was rapidly approaching. In this strait, I looked around for the nearest place of shelter, and seeing a thin column of smoke curling up from the depths of a gorge apparently but a short distance off, I turned my steps in that direction. Clambering down the mountain-side with much difficulty, when near the bottom, my course was arrested by a bold rivulet, which went dashing and foaming over its rocky bed, making an insuperable barrier to my further progress. It was too late to turn back; I was fearful of losing my way, and thinking it safest to follow the course of the stream, I groped along through the thick copse in search of a crossing. I had gone but a little way, when a treacherous stone slipping under my foot, I lost my balance and fell over the bank into the torrent. I remember feeling one pang of excruciating pain, and then all was dark. When I awoke to consciousness, I was lying on a couch in a dimly lighted room. Two persons were standing by the bedside—a man and a woman. 'Holy Virgin! be praised,' I heard the man say in a whisper, and in the Italian tongue, 'he lives; the tea, Joanna.' He placed a chalice to my lips, and I swallowed the contents, which were not ungrateful to the taste, at a draught. What the decoction was, I know not; but its effect was magical. In a twinkling I was so much revived as to ask where I was and how I came there. I was told that I was at the manse of the curé of a neighboring hamlet; that luckily the noise I made in falling into the water caught the ear of a dog at a chalêt close by, whose baying brought some shepherds to my rescue. By them I was extricated and conveyed to the manse in a senseless condition. I was nearly drowned, but otherwise my injuries were not serious—a sprained ankle and several painful bruises made up the catalogue. My good physician, the curé, assured me that I would be well taken care of, and bade me be quiet for the rest of the night, which injunction he reinforced by giving me a composing elixir of some kind. Next morning I was well enough to leave my bed, although disabled from walking by the injury to my foot. There was nothing to do but to wait patiently for it to heal before pursuing my journey, and to this lot I was easily reconciled on finding in my host not only a kind and skillful leach, but a most agreeable and interesting companion. The spot itself was very attractive, and the window of my room looked out on a romantic scene. A short distance from the house the rivulet widened into a lake some miles in extent, which was completely engirdled by mountains. On the opposite side, perched upon a lofty crag, was a half-ruined castle, a relic of the feudal times. This is so common an object in that country, that it soon ceases to attract the attention of the tourist. Each has its store of dark and dismal legends, which the cicerone recounts with hideous sameness of circumstance and detail. Of course the castle across the lake was no exception; but having supped full with supernatural horrors, I felt little inclination to learn its history. For that reason, I was not prepared to hear that it had recently been the scene of a tragedy of the most harrowing description.

"It was the morning of the day I had fixed upon for my departure. I was sitting on a bench in the garden reading, when the curé came to me. I saw from his countenance that he had something of more than ordinary interest to impart, and putting aside my book, turned toward him inquiringly, as he seated himself by my side. 'Doubtless,' he began, 'you think it was what short-sighted mortals call an accident that turned your steps hither; am I not right?' The question took me by sur-

9*

prise. I replied, that while I believed that all our acts were directed by an over-ruling Providence, yet, not having the gift of prophecy, I was unable to discern what there was of special significance in the event to which he referred. 'You are wise, my son,' said he, 'to cast from you the Atheist's doctrine of blind chance; every word and deed of men, casual and light as they may seem, have an everlasting import for good or evil; are entered up on one side or the other of the dread account book of eternity. It was the hand of God that guided you to this place, for a purpose which I will presently explain. One night last March, while a snow storm was raging, the shepherds at the chalêt on yonder mountain were aroused by the loud baying of a dog, and going to see what was the matter, found a man in a helpless condition not a stone's throw from the spot of your misadventure. In obedience to my standing injunction, they brought him at once to the manse. He was the veriest wretch my eyes ever beheld, the merest shadow of a human being in the last stage of misery. I did all in my power to restore him, but my efforts were fruitless. After lingering a fortnight, he died of simple inanition. Before breathing his last, he confessed himself of a crime which made my blood run cold; he was the victim of remorse. I had great difficulty in understanding his broken and, at times, incoherent narrative; but this was the substance of it. The man was a Neapolitan, a servant of Don Jacapo Torella, whose family is one of the most wealthy and powerful in that kingdom. This man, the master, was such a villain as only can be found in that land where Satan holds undisputed dominion. He had an uncle, Don Lelio Torella, a virtuous, good man, whose dwelling there was as solitary as Lot's in Sodom. He was of a somewhat eccentric disposition; had been liberally educated; was fond of letters and the company of learned men, and led a retired life at his villa near the city. By his tact and abilities he had contrived for a long time to keep clear of political broils, and to maintain a strict neutrality in the struggles of contending factions. He was a bachelor; with him lived his niece, the only child of a sister, whose husband, Eustace Conrad, was killed in the affair of Villetri, fighting on the side of Germany. He was of Saubian origin, as his name implied, and was of royal descent. The policy of Charles the Bourbon, then King of Naples, was to conciliate all classes of the old nobility and higher orders, and he so far succeeded in this as to draw even the inveterate Don Lelio from his retirement, and persuade him to take office at the court. Here his caustic wit and haughty bearing kept him in hot water with the prime minister, who was a man of narrow views, of plebian origin, and head of the third estate—then beginning to exert a controlling influence in public affairs. There was at that time a young officer attached to the garrison of Castle Nuovo, who was a special favorite of the king; he was known as Don Henri Campabello. He was of English parentage, and had entered the service of Naples as an adventurer, or soldier of fortune. He was described as a man of extraordinary personal graces, strangely contrasting with those of his own rank by whom he was surrounded.

"'The King was an ardent sportsman, and in his hunting excursions Campabello was his inseparable companion. As was to be expected, this marked preference of the sovereign for the society of a foreigner was very distasteful to the native chivalry, with all of whom, except his comrades-in-arms, he was in constant danger of open rupture. There was another person in whose eyes the young officer found particular favor; this was Constance Conrad, the beautiful niece of Don Lelio, and it was soon apparent that the old nobleman, too, regarded him with far more esteem than he did any other of her numerous suitors.

"'In course of time, Don Lelio fell into trouble at court, having quarreled violently with Tanucci, the premier, and in a fit of displeasure retired to his villa. Campabello's rivals, chief of whom was Don Jacapo Torella, now redoubled their efforts to degrade him in the king's estimation, and with the aid of the all-powerful minister, so far succeeded as to prevail with Charles to order him away to a distant garrison on the plausible pretext of its being a more honorable station. But before the king's command was made known to Campabello, it was discovered that he had been secretly married to Constance at the instance of Don Lelio, who was resolved to disappoint the schemes of his relatives, whom he detested, while at the same time he dreaded their enmity. The discovery was the signal of the terrible troubles which followed in rapid succession. On some frivolous accusation, easily invented in that country of diabolical plots, Don Lelio was rudely seized and thrown into the dungeons of the Vicaria, and shortly afterwards Campabello and his wife, with their infant child, disappeared from the scene of thickening dangers. Aware of the implacable nature of their enemies, they took every precaution to conceal their retreat. Whither they fled was known only to one trusty servant, who insisted upon sharing their lot. Alas! that this poor, devoted friend should have been the innocent cause of the mischief which afterwards ensued.

"'Campabello and his wife were naturally much concerned about the fate of Don Lelio. After the lapse of two months, no longer able to restrain their anxiety, they despatched their attendant, Guillame, on a secret mission to Naples for news. The messenger returned in safety, but he brought with him the worst tidings their fears foreboded. The old nobleman did not long survive the brutal outrage to which he had been subjected, and Don Jacapo had fallen heir to his possessions. Time rolled on. The child, a boy, was now a year old; it is said that he closely resembled his mother, and was exceeding beautiful. He was watched over with jealous vigilance by his parents; and, though they had implicit confidence in his nurse, she was seldom permitted to take him out of doors. One day she went to walk with the child and never more returned. For days search was made for them without avail. At last the body of the woman was discovered floating in the water a short distance from the castle.'

"'The castle!' I involuntarily exclaimed.

"'At the foot of the high rock you see there on the right of that old ruin is where they found her, but there was no trace of the child. His loss was a fatal blow to Lady Campabello, and soon after her death the castle was deserted. This much of the story was current among the villagers when I came here to reside. There was no talk among them of foul play. It was generally believed that the body of the child was at the bottom of the deep lake, into which the nurse had, as they surmised, accidentally fallen. Imagine, then, my horror, when this poor wretch, in accents scarcely audible, told how he had penetrated Guillame's disguise, and thus discovered the retreat of the fugitives; how he had been hired for a large price to avenge his master by slaying his hated rival; how, foiled in that, he thought he could appease his master's wrath by stealing the child, and how, in carrying out that fell design, he had hurled the poor woman headlong over the precipice into the lake before she could cry out and give the alarm. He carried the boy to Naples; but instead of the reward he expected, he was loaded with curses, and scourged from his master's presence.

"'What shall he do in this extremity? It is a desperate alternative; yet he is resolved to make one more effort to regain his master's favor. He makes his way back to the neighborhood of the castle, taking the child with him. He finds it deserted; he learns the lady's fate; sudden and swift the awful retribution comes; terror and remorse have seized upon him. Vile and desperate as he was, he had no thought of harming the child; indeed, a strange revulsion of feeling now possessed him—he could have no peace of mind until he had found the father, and restored the child to him. Where to look for him? While he was lurking around the castle, he, one night, caught fragments of a conversation between the young officer and his wife, in which he spoke of going to France, to some place near Grenoble. Going thither, he could learn nothing of the object of his pursuit. He left the child in the care of a peasant woman, living near an old chateau, and went on to Paris. Here his evil genius involved him in a serious affray, in consequence of which he was condemned to imprisonment for life.

"'After three years of confinement, he made his escape. His first thought, on regaining liberty, was of the child. He hastened back to the place where he had left it; it was gone; the woman was dead, and all he could learn of the child was that it had been carried away by a stranger—a priest—no one could tell whither. Then he gave up to despair. He became a vagabond upon the earth, and wandering distractedly hither and thither, at last is drawn by some mysterious impulse back to the scene of his inexpiable crime. Ere he reaches it, the blinding tempest rushes down upon him and smites him senseless to the earth. How he was found has been told. He had barely finished his terrible story, when he fell back on his couch and expired. I had listened to many a tale of human suffering and crime, but nothing in all my experience affected me as did the confession of this miserable man. It was ever in my mind, and I

lived from day to day in the hope of hearing what
had become of the father and child. The mother's
grave is in the village churchyard; I had frequently
visited it before, but now it was invested with
peculiar sanctity. I went there two and three times
every week, always expecting that somebody interested in the unhappy pair would come to inquire
for them. Time passed. I had begun to feel that
my hope was vain, when one morning, towards the
end of June, on repairing, as usual, to the ceme-
tery, I was startled by the sight of a man standing beside the grave of Constance. He leant heavily
upon his staff, and his bare head was bent down in
prayer. His garments were threadbare and travel-
stained, and he carried a knapsack strapped to his
shoulders. He was old, and, when in a little while,
he turned to go away, I saw that, although his
carriage was erect, his step was slow and feeble.
I spoke to him. He stopped, and seeing who I
was, saluted me respectfully. It was Guillame. I
took him home with me, and when he was rested
and refreshed, made him tell his story. Briefly, it
was this: The morning after Lady Constance was
consigned to the tomb, Campabello said to him,
"We must part, Guillame; I am going away."
Throwing himself at his feet, the faithful creature
implored his master, with tears, not to dismiss him.
Campabello was deeply touched. "So be it," he said.
"In an hour we start for St. Petersburg." Here let
me explain what was the secret of Guillame's
attachment to the young Englishman. He had been
a soldier in the company which Campabello commanded. On one occasion, a subaltern struck him

with his sword for some fancied dereliction of duty.
Incensed by the wanton outrage, he gave the officer a blow in return with the butt of his musket,
which killed him outright. For this offence, he
was condemned to die, and the sentence would have
been executed but for the intercession of Campabello, who obtained a pardon for him from the
king.

"'Arrived at their destination, the young officer
was kindly received by the Czar, and readily given
a commission in the Imperial army. His stay at
the capital was as short as ceremony permitted.
Desiring to be at once actively employed, he was
ordered to the frontier. Here, in time, he won rep-
utation and honors in abundance. Ambitious of
distinction, and ardently devoted to the profession
of arms, he was in the full tide of a brilliant
career, when, on a sudden, his health succumbed
to the rigors of that inhospitable climate. His
death severed the last tie which bound Guillame
to earthly objects. He felt that his own end was
not far off, and yearning to look once more on his
native sky before closing his eyes forever, he had,
with toil and pain, plodded his way back to this
spot. His prayer had been granted, and now he
was ready to die, and wished to be buried at the
feet of his mistress. I told him the valet's story;
he was amazed and shocked beyond description.
Next morning he came to me equipped for a journey—his knapsack on his back and staff in hand;
said he was going in search of the child. His dear
mistress had appeared to him in a dream in her
angelic robes, telling him that little Edward was

10

alive, and commanding him to go without delay. It was an idle fantasy, but I knew it was useless to oppose his determination. He went, I fear, never to return. You came, or rather, you were brought here more dead than alive. Hearing you speak, I recognized your country in your voice. You were come, I thought, in search of the lost ones. I was mistaken; yet you were directed hither by the Divine Power as the means of bringing it all to light. Is that not plain?'

"Father Manso's narrative made a deep impression on me. The more I reflected on it, the more earnest became the desire to discover the fate of the poor orphan. Yet it seemed to my view an almost hopeless undertaking, and I so expressed myself concerning it to the good man, whose zeal in the matter awakened my warmest sympathy. I had no idea, I said, who the English nobleman was. There were ever so many of my countrymen (I did not think it worth while to undeceive him as to my nativity), abroad in Europe, especially in France. I had met one or more of them at every stage of my travels; but of this one, I had not the least inkling. 'Stay,' said the priest; 'I had nearly forgotten it; look at this.' He drew from his bosom a gold watch, and opening the case handed it to me. I read the engraving, "To Henry Markham, from his uncle Edward." 'That watch,' continued the curé, 'was entrusted to me by Guillame before he went away; it was given to him by his master on his death bed. Now, at least, you know what was the officer's name.' 'Yes,' said I, repeating the inscription aloud; 'but it affords no

clue to the missing child; if it did, I should spare
no pains or sacrifice in following it up. As it
was, we were groping in total darkness. I could
only engage to do the best I could under the circumstances.' 'Go, then, my son,' said he, 'and
God's blessing attend you.'

"That evening I set out to return to Geneva.
Thence, in a few days, I started for France, traveling through Savoy. On the way I fell ill. I
managed, with difficulty, to reach the monastery of
Grande Chartreuse, which I had visited once before.
There I was tenderly cared for through the severest
illness I have ever experienced. When the fever
left me, I became the prey of the worst dread
which can possess the wanderer in a strange land,
and as soon as I was strong enough to travel, I
turned my face homeward. Yet I did not wholly
forget my promise to Father Manso. As it lay
near my route, I went to the place where the
miscreant had left the child. The information I
obtained only went to confirm his account. The
chateau was ruinous and desolate enough. Nobody
had lived there, I was told, since the old lord,
one Count de Villieures, died, in what year my
informant did not remember."

CHAPTER X.

"READ on, Dick," said Carleton, as Alloway paused.

"That's all there is," said he. "Uncle had great repugnance to speak of his own sufferings. He had, indeed, been sick well nigh unto death, and his frame was so shattered by it, that he was fearful he would not be able to reach home. He told mother how intensely anxious he was, and how fervently he prayed that he might be suffered to lay his weary burden down on the spot where his pilgrimage begun."

"It is that thought which has ever embittered the last hour of the poor exile," replied Carleton, with feeling. "*Dulce moriens reminisciter Argos.*"

Both were silent for several minutes. At length Dick said:

"You have heard the story, Harry, what do you think of it?"

Harry—"Oh, its well enough as far as it goes; indeed, could not be better for a story, as you say; but it is not much to the point. Campabello! that's Italian for Campbell. Mrs. Graeme was a Campbell, was she not?"

Dick.—"Yes; the clan is legion."

Harry.—"But you told me Mrs. Graeme did not talk like a Scotchwoman.

Dick.—"She was educated in England, I believe. The fact is, I know just nothing at all about her early history; yet I'll be sworn that she has no more to do with that Mr. Conrad and his affairs than the man in the moon."

Harry.—"It may be so; but how do you account for her husband's strange speech?"

Alloway made no reply.

Harry.—"More mystery, Dickon, my boy; the plot thickens, and I am more bent than ever on getting to the bottom of it. Aye," he exclaimed, springing from the sofa, and glaring in true stage fashion at an imaginary apparition, "I'll follow thee, thou ghost or goblin damned, though thou leadest me to the Stygian caves forlorn, 'mid sights and sounds and shrieks unholy!"

Alloway laughed heartily.

"What a muddle you are making of Milton and Shakespeare! Psha, Harry, let the *parlez-vousing*—"

"Buccaneer," suggested his friend, seeing him pause for a word.

"Anything you like, so you send him packing about his business, and proceed to tell me more of your grand military project. Bravo! that's the look —every inch a soldier—in a dressing-gown! See how his bosom glows, and how he pants for the glorious fray; how he smelleth the battle afar off; the thunder of the captains and the shouting. *Vincere est vivere!* that's the motto for a true hero."

A remarkable change had indeed come over the

10*

volatile spirits of the youthful cavalier. His handsome face was lighted up with strange animation; the languid air and light, bantering tone were gone, and he was pacing the floor with quick and nervous steps.

"You misjudge me greatly, my dear friend," he instantly replied, in a somewhat excited and impassioned tone of voice, "if you think I am ambitious of military renown, and long for the fame which is to be gathered in the dreadful field of revolution. Believe me, I do not aspire after the trophies which are won only at the frightful cost of human blood shed in deadly conflict. In my ears the sound of the trumpet is a summons to the carnival of death, rousing in every bosom the 'spirit of the first-born Cain.' War, unless it is waged in defence of our country, our altars and household gods, is cool, deliberate, organized, wholesale murder. In the dark ages, the soldier's trade was the one honorable profession. The sword was the universal arbiter of disputes, the certain badge of nobility, the true emblem of dignity and power; prowess in arms was the only guerdon worthy of attainment. But feudalism was unmitigated barbarism, a scene of perpetual strife, rapine, anarchy; a saturnalia of blood, a horrible orgy of crimes of the darkest hue. The institution of knighthood was the only partial gleam of humanity athwart the black sky; a feeble, glimmering ray of light rendering the darkness more profound. You seem to be looking into an immense, murky cavern of embattled fiends, realizing Milton's description of the abode of the damned. The necessity for an extra judicial

mode of repressing cruelty and redressing wrongs is
the strongest proof of the degeneracy of the race.
By the laws of their order, these martial custodians of society and vindicators of the sacred claims
of honor and chastity were bound themselves to
respect the obligations whose violation they so rig-
orously punished in others; but although they miti-
gated, in some degree, the ferocity of men, they did
not succeed in redeeming the world from the
dominion of brute violence. Nay, the ensigns armo-
rial of this boasted chivalry are crimson dyed with
the gore of innocent victims of fanatical zeal and
romantic enthusiasm—euphumisms for licentious passion and ungovernable rage—sanctified lust, canonized
murder. *Tantum religio potuit saudere malorum!*
Godfrey of ᛫ Bouillon led his band of consecrated
assassins on to pillage and massacre in sight of
Calvary, and years afterwards, on the same holy
ground, Richard the Lion-hearted learned his first
lessons in the quality of that mercy 'which becometh
the throned monarch better than his crown' from
the noble example of a Moslem prince."

"Shade of La Mancha! what shall be done with
this profane iconoclast?" cried Alloway, as Carleton
paused in his flight to rest the wings of his eloquence. "Oh, that I were such an orator as Bru-
tus is!"

"Orator? God forbid!" said Carleton. "One
trumpeter of the name will do; it is high time
some of us were signalizing our zeal in acts, and
I glory in being the first to set the example. There
is no lack of splendid talkers among us; they are
as plentiful as lawyers of old in Naples. What-

ever you do, my friend, I entreat you will not write me down among the *homines inertissimi, quorum omnis vis virtusque in lingua sita est.*"

Dick.—"Orator or not, you 'hae sae saft a voice and slid a tongue,' that you can say three words to my one. But I have yonder an authority will confound your awful invective. Read what Dr. Robertson says in commendation of mediæval chivalry in his last great work—the 'History of the Reign of Charles V.'"

Harry.—"I have read carefully every word of the book. History has been my chief study of late; especially everything relating to the abominations of feudal despotism. Robertson's laudation of this creature of military genius for its lasting beneficial influence on the manners and customs of a barbarous age, is all leather and prunella. Think of his saying that the germ of modern as distinguished from ancient civilization is contained in the bond of knight-erranty. Why, sir, civilization owes more to the humble mechanic of Mentz than to all the mitres, sceptres and swords of Christendom. The PRINTING PRESS was the mighty engine which battered down the walls of arbitrary power and freed the soul from the bondage of ignorance, error and superstition. To this art of arts are due the ameliorations of human society—all those grand reformations which are now in process of fulfillment; in the institutions of policy; in the canons of religious doctrine and belief; in the essential principles of jurisprudence and the enlightened precepts of government, no less than in the countless appliances of industry and wealth—in everything that humanizes, elevates, refines and adorns human character."

"Well for you," said Dick, taking advantage of a pause in Carleton's oration to edge in a word, "that you did not live in the days of old Sir William Berkeley; he would have hung you higher than Haman for that audacious speech."

"Hold your tongue, Dick," rejoined his companion. "As I was going to remark, I am free to admit that originally the word chivalry was meant to denote the acme of manly virtue, the supreme ideal of private worth, public zeal and religious devotion. But soon the honor of knighthood became a purely arbitrary distinction; a conventional charter of exclusive personal privileges; a merely factitious order of so-called nobility. It was no more prized as the reward of true merit, of courage tempered with gentleness and Christian courtesy; no longer was it the sure evidence of substantial claims to spotless renown. No, it now became the paltry, unprized gift of princely favor; a thing of accident, a toy, a bauble; its lustre dimmed by brutal excesses, and its guerdons the insignia of tyrannical power."

Here Alloway made a desperate effort to rally to the defence of the abused paladins, but he was borne down by the sweeping torrent of Carleton's harangue.

"As for the protection afforded the weaker sex, the refinements of gallantry and all that sort of Sydnean rhodomontade, the charter of knighthood was not the first recognition of the righful province of woman, nor admission of the benignant influence of her gentle sway in curbing the headstrong passions and softening the rugged asperities of savage man. This uncouth gallantry was a sentimental, spasmodical worship of the impersonations of phrenzied fancy, not the natural spontaneous feeling of devotion, love and deference for creatures endowed with charms and graces which make them the living fountains of the choicest blessings of society. Let us give the old paladins credit for the best intentions in their ungainly schemes of reformation; but in the name of true manhood, let us at the same time protest that it was not a marvellous display of heroic virtue to shield helpless beauty from insult and violence, and to render that homage no generous heart could refuse to *la belle sexe*. And then their immaculate tribunal of justice, their sublime code of honor, their amazing discovery that truth was a Phrygian puzzle which only the sword could unravel. It ought to be enough among Christian people to know that duelling is condemned by the word of God. But examine it on merely human grounds. It is claimed to be the only honorable method of disposing of mortal quarrels between man and man. A combat to be honorable must be fair and equal, and everybody knows that it is practically impossible to put the belligerents on such terms that the advantage will not be greatly in favor of one or the other of them. The challenged party, who is generally most in the wrong, is allowed the choice of weapons, and, unless he be wholly indifferent to the issue, is sure to select the death-dealing instrument with which he is most familiar. But what moral right have you to require the injured or aggrieved party to forego any superiority he may possess? What rule of justice demands that you should take your adversary's weapons, or even advise him with what sort of artillery you purpose to fight? Think of David's sending Goliah word that he was coming forth to battle armed with a sling and five smooth stones out of the brook, and thereby giving the ugly giant a chance to collect a magazine of boulders and bombard him to death at long range. If men will resort to this sanguinary mode of accommodating disputes, if only blood can wash out the stains of affronted dignity, then assuredly a decent respect for social obligations plainly dictates that the combatants should end the matter with as little ado as possible, and whatever may be the result of the fight, the least said about honor the better. Honor can never be vindicated by bloody reprisals, any more than the blazonry of chivalrous deeds can ennoble the perpetrators of cruel injustice. At the best, what merit is there in being accounted a skillful or a fortunate duellist? It is not Harry Monmouth exulting over the fallen Percy, stooping to pluck the budding honors from that noble crest to make a garland for his own, who appears grandly heroic, but Harry the King, as he is pictured by the divine artist on the night before Agincourt—

> "'Upon his royal face there is no note
> How dread an army hath surrounded him,
> Nor doth he dedicate one jot of color
> Unto the weary and all-watched night;
> But freshly looks and overbears attaint
> With cheerful semblance and sweet majesty,
> That every wretch, pining and pale before,
> Beholding him, plucks comfort from his looks—
> A largess universal like the sun,
> His liberal eye doth give to every one,
> Thawing cold fear.' '

Having rendered this magnificent quotation in a
way that Garrick or John Kemble could not have
excelled, Carleton subsided into his former recum-
bency with the lackadaisical and *insouciant* air of
one to whom such oratorical flourishes were—

"No more difficile
Than for pig to squeal or blackbird to whistle."

"Jupiter Tonans!" exclaimed Alloway, "what a
Vesuvius of eloquence. And all this tirade because
I happened to say that you had the bearing of a
soldier, longing to flush his maiden sword. I recant,
Harry. After all, fighting is a wretched trade, and
for one, I am willing to forego my share of its
gory and grinning honors. Excuse me for quoting
Shakespeare, but it is my highest aspiration—

"'To live the lease of nature and pay my breath
To time and mortal custom.'

"Whatever your wise saws may say, death is an
ugly customer, come when and how he will; and none
the more welcome because he has a churlish habit
of coming unasked and undesired. Then, for the
glory of the thing, what is there to choose between
the laureled crown of the 'hook-nosed fellow of
Rome,' and the scalp-locks of various hues which
deck the robe of the mighty king of the Wampa-
noags? And as for those great, hulky bullies of
the grand carousal, sheathed all over in 'helm and
hauberk's twisted mail,' sword and lance proof,
what were their wrought-iron pastimes, their jousts
and tourneys, compared with the robust and plucky
rencontres of the old gladiators of the Coliseum,
who went at it, stripped to the buff, and hacked

the flesh off each other until nothing was left of
them but a bloody array of skeleton warriors rattling defiance to death itself? But, sir, do you
wish to see my perfect model of a fighting animal?
Behold him in the wrathful, red fiend of the wilderness, accoutred for the war-path; the incarnation of real chivalry in naked majesty. Talk of
Grecian, Roman, Saxon or Celtic courage and fortitude—

"'Believe me, prince, there is not an *Indian*
That traverses our vast *American* deserts
In quest of prey and lives upon his bow,
But better practices these boasted virtues.'

"*Pour vivre en se-fait tuer,* is the motto of the
killing trade the world over. Between the hero
and the brute it is but a toss-up, as you were saying, Harry."

Carlton did not deign to notice this unseemly
badinage; so Dick picked his flint, and began blazing away at him again.

"O, for the genius of Moliere! what a comedy
I would indite. *Le soldat malgre lui,* worth an
army of your mock doctors; a veritable hero, whose
natal star was the serenest of the heavenly orbs.
For a surety, my Harry is not that famous 'Hotspur of the North,' he that kills me some six or
seven dozen of Scots at a breakfast."

This time the shot told; Carlton was half angry.

"You certainly can make yourself supremely ridiculous when you try, you great, hairy jack-pudding,"
he exclaimed, snatching up the poker and making a
feint as if he were going to run Dick through the
body with it. "You know well enough that what I

11

have said was not intended to decry the profession of
arms, nor to underrate the military art. Nobody
appreciates the character of a true soldier higher
than I do. The unsullied honors which are won
in the field of duty are above the price of rubies;
he does not deserve to be called a man who turns
his back on his country's foes. But the mercenary
wretch whose sword is up for hire; the blood-
thirsty creature who fights for the mere love of
fighting, who delights in war for war's sake, as
Xenophon says of Clearchus—"

"Are all a vile, murderous crew at the best," said
Dick; "the moral of all your fine talk is, that wars,
like plagues and earthquakes, are unavoidable calamities, and therefore the soldier's vocation will never
be out of fashion. Well, as Corporal Nym says,
'things must be as they may.' Don't mind my chaf-
fing, Harry; I know you will act your part as
becomes a right valiant rebel, whether you like the
business or not. But, I say, when did the Carle-
tons get to be such a rebellious set? the name once
stood for loyalty itself."

Harry.—"Loyalty, forsooth! First tell me what
makes a rebel before you impugn my loyalty, as
you call it."

"What makes a rebel?" slowly repeated Dick;
"strange that I never thought seriously of that
question before. To be a rebel one must have com-
mitted treason in some way. But what is treason?
It strikes me that Harrington made a palpable hit
in his famous couplet—

"'Treason doth never prosper, what's the reason,
For if it prosper, none dare call it treason.'

Harry.—"Precisely so; and hence loyalty is a noun Proteus, which no lexicographer has ever been able to define."

Dick.—"Wait till old 'Taxation-no-Tyranny' publishes the second edition of his dictionary, and we shall have your *Proteus* 'drained in a limbec to his native form.' For example: *Loyalty*—a term employed to denote that overpowering sensation of awe and reverence which is inspired by the contemplation of the divinity which doth hedge a king. But we are going to succeed in this struggle, and then we can have a vocabulary of our own, which will put to shame the servile coiners of words who would call a whale a weasel at the bidding of any Royal Dane."

Carleton laughed.

"Glibly said, for orator Mum. Now that he has shaken the reefs out of his rhetorical sails, he has completely taken the wind out of mine."

"And when the muss is over, and we are a free, independent, and supremely happy people," continued Dick, with renewed volubility, "what are we going to do next? There's the rub. I should go for a monarchy if I were sure of a dukedom for myself. If it is to be a republic, then let us have the strongest possible infusion of the aristocratical element. I confess I am, for one, no admirer of pure and unadulterated democracy, and regret to see that some of our state cooks are for putting so much of that sort of leaven in our political loaf."

Harry.—"The current of opinion sets overwhelmingly in favor of a republic. I wish you could see the letters my father has received from every quarter on this subject, especially those from Col. George Mason and Mr. Samuel Adams. There is no disputing the fact that the republican form of government is the choice of this generation of Americans. If posterity don't like it, why let posterity make one to suit themselves."

Leaving these young rebels to their dish of politics, let us direct the reader's attention to some of the other persons of our drama.

CHAPTER XI.

BY a singular combination of circumstances, it so happens that the anniversary of Miss Lucy Graeme's nativity is one of the days in our story's calendar most crowded with stirring incidents. Despite the evil prediction of the immemorial weather prophet, the dawn we celebrate came not in heavy with clouds and lowering with gloomy forebodings, but was robed in a dreamy mantle of heavenly radiance, which made every object appear as though it dwelt in a perpetual realm of drowsy-headed illusion. Yet it was in reality no fairy-land of shadowy images, enchanting visions and "dreams that wave before the half-shut eye"; on the contrary, it was a breathing, throbbing part of that grand theatre whose curtain was about to rise on the swelling scene of the world's supremest hopes.

As we were saying, the eventful day was come, and Bonhill resounded with the busy note of preparation. It is the little lady-regent's first essay at entertaining on so large a scale, and she duly appreciates the weight of responsibility which rests on her pretty shoulders. Trying as the situation is, enough to tax the resources of the most experienced adept in the occult science of housekeeping, we have no sort of misgiving that she will not come off with flying colors from the field of her unwonted labors.

Returning from his customary morning ride, Mr. Graeme found the house, as he would say, turned "heels-owre-gowdie" from attic to cellar. Everywhere the genius of distraction reigned supreme. Even the paternal sanctum had not escaped the invasion of the common enemy of peace and quiet; it was undergoing a complete overhauling and setting to rights, preparatory to being dedicated to a variety of unheard of uses, and especially for the behoof of those elderly persons who preferred a rubber at whist or a game of vingt-un to the boisterous attractions of fiddling and dancing. Only his wife's chamber was sacred ground; but the self-respect of the worthy gentleman revolted at the notion of being held a prisoner in his own castle, and calling after the boy who was leading his horse to the stable, he determined to make his exit from the scene of domestic din and disorder. As he was leaving the hall with that view, he was intercepted by his daughter, who came tripping up to him with an open letter in her hand, and in the most aggravating manner actually carolling a stave of one of his favorite songs.

"Nae luck about the house!" he exclaimed, taking the words from her mouth, and trying his best to preserve an awkward assumption of outraged dignity. "Is this yer manners, to drive a body out o' doors with your clatter and skirling eneugh to distrackit auld Nick; and he yer ain dear faither."

"I am sure the poor, persecuted body could make himself very comfortable up-stairs in mother's room," was the provoking reply to his grievous complaint.

"In yer mither's room; a douce answer to a ceevil question. Hech, sirs! a pretty pass, the head o' the family maunna hae his ain seat in his ain house. That gate belyve I shall be e'en begging your leddyship's permission to wear my ain breecks. What are ye snirtling at, ye little imp o' the deil? Let me catch ye grinning at me again, an' I'll gie ye that will gar ye laugh out o' the wrang side o' your mouth."

The threat was aimed at the luckless urchin who had brought the letter for Lucy from Clifton, and who was detected in a broad grimace at what he seemed to think was very rare fun.

"Alack, alack!" cried Lucy, catching him by the lappel of his coat, and looking up at him in a commiserating way, "how I do pity the poor head of the family; if he is well nigh daft at the clatter and skirling of the scrubbing-brush, what will become of him when he hears the dinsome clamor of the dancing and deray to-night?

> "'The cushat croods, the corbie cries,
> The cuckoo couks, the prattling pies
> To keek hir they begin;
> The jargon o' the jangling jays,
> The craiking craws, the keekling kayes,
> They deaved me with their din.'"

An apt representation of the melodious discord one hears in a room full of gay revellers, all laughing and talking in an undistinguishable jumble of hilarious sounds, and she recited it with such humorous effect that Mr. Graeme's sides fairly shook with laughter in spite of his efforts to maintain his gravity. Yet there was a mischievous twinkle in his eye as he chimed in with his daughter's merry mood.

"Hout tout, lass," he exclaimed, as soon as he had recovered his breath; "gang awa wi' your daffin. Ye dinna really suppose that I care a bodle mysel for your noise and dirdum and a' that; I was only just the moment thinking what the gude minister will hae to say anent the matter; he'll be sair mistrysted, I hae nae doubt, at sic a sight o' wardly vanity."

Instantly the tables were turned; the mischief-loving damsel was transformed as if by magic into a ludicrous picture of mingled consternation and chagrin.

"Goodness sake! papa, you don't mean to tell me that Mr. Waddell is coming to-night?" she faltered out.

The old gentleman made no reply in words, he merely shook his head solemnly sideways and down-ways, as the sly twinkle lurking in his eye grew more and more intolerably wicked. To account for this sudden revulsion of feeling on Miss Lucy's part, it is necessary to remark that Mr. Waddell was the famous "new-light" preacher, who, it had been given out, would hold forth in the parish church on the next Sunday, and who was expected to make his quarters at Bonhill towards the close of the week. Now, there had never been a dissent-ing minister in that immediate neighborhood within

the memory of the oldest inhabitant, and the preva-
lent opinion of such a character was far from flattering, or expressed in very reverential or even
respectful terms. He was generally looked upon to
be sour, peevish, cross and splenetic, with an elon-
gated, kill-joy visage, a harsh, whining voice, which
"entuned in the nose full swetely," and with a
garb to match these prepossessing endowments of
the most puritanical pattern. With all her respect
for her father's pronounced religious predilections,
Lucy had been insensibly impressed by the obnox-
ious popular description of the itinerant preacher of
the period, and the idea of having one of the number in the house on a day which had been set
apart for festivity and jollification was anything but
pleasant to contemplate. Then she knew that Mr.
Graeme would be mortified beyond measure if his
visitor was not agreeably lodged and entertained
with the exemplary courtesy and respectful attention which was due to his sacred calling, and she
was naturally apprehensive concerning his reception
at the hands of the more thoughtless of the gay
company, who might be disposed to resent the
presence of a rigid presbyter as "an infusion of
myrrh into the festive goblet." No wonder, then,
that she was dismayed at the suggestion of Mr.
Waddell's intrusion on the scene of pleasure, and
looked as if she was ready to cry with vexation.
Mr. Graeme's heart melted at sight of her extreme
discomfiture.

"Dinna greet, lassie," said he, kissing her affectionately; "ye maunna mind my daffin. The minister will na come before to-morrow e'en, so Jamie

Gordon writes. What hae ye got there?" he asked, glancing at the letter in her hand.

"It's only a line from Mary Littleton," replied Lucy, "to inquire when the *Katrine* will sail.'

Mr. Graeme pricked up his ears at this announcement, but his countenance immediately fell as she added:

"The information is particularly desired by the strange gentleman."

"The strange gentleman?" he sneeringly repeated; "I dinna ken why he's aye speerin' after the vessel."

"That's Mr. Conrad's affair, my dear sir," retorted Lucy, who had not yet forgiven him his cruel joke. "What answer shall I make to the polite request of your *bubbly-jock*, for such he certainly appears to be from the way you speak of him."

Again her father laughed heartily. The popular anecdote of the half-witted gowk who had such a mortal fear of the great, gobbling turkey-cock was one of his jocular stand-bys.

"The unnatural bairn," he exclaimed, "aye shootin' at her auld faither wi' his ain gun. Ye mind the story then? But what gars ye think I am sair hadden doun by the bubbly-jock?"

"Because," was the unexpectedly round response, "you give yourself more concern about him than I can see any reason for."

Mr. Graeme's face reddened a little at his daughter's bluntness; but his displeasure, if he really felt any, vanished the moment he met her rallying glance.

"Weel, weel, lass," said he, "ye are na far wrang;

it's sinfu' idling o' precious time, if it is naething
warse. Sae, ye maun, just tell the young leddie or
the ——."

"Bubbly-jock," said Lucy.

"Gentleman," continued her father, with reprov-
ing emphasis on the word; "wi' my respectful
compliments, that the *Katrine* will set sail on the
first fair wind after twal o'clock the night, and he
kens when that will be precisely as weel as mysel."

"That does not sound like a polite message,
papa."

"It is een word for word as I got it frae your
cousin Ballantine at the store a while gone; but
say it to suit yoursel. And now I am minded to
ask, did you add the postscript to the letter to
Geordie?"

"Yes, sir," replied Lucy, "every word as you
desired it—the message about the model of the new
steam engine, and the threshing machine, and all;
and I also requested him to send me the latest
collection of songs—the one just published in Edin-
burgh."

"A' right eneugh," said her father; "yet how
you will get them is anither question. The *Katrine*,
I am afraid, is the last vessel we shall see frae
the auld countree these mony lang and weary days.
It gars me grew to think on't. A waefu warld.
It's aye the way o' it, thae folk wha hae maist
cause to be freenly and Christianlike and forbear-
ing in a' their dealings with ain anither, are the
vera ones to fall out and gae to hacking ilk ithers
thrapples anent the right and the wrang o' this and
that metapheesical abstraiction, so that there is

never an end o' contention, and strife, and blood-
shed, and destruction. I hae. my ain gude opinion
on the subject; but wha's the use arguing wi' a
wheen het-headed callants wha will na hearken to
rhyme or reason? I maun as weel, as the saying
is, keep my breath to cool my parritch. Ane ither
thing, you sent the invitations to the gentlemen
whase names I gave you?"

"I did, papa," said Lucy; "although I was
doubtful of the propriety of asking Mr. Thompson
to the party; his politics, you know—"

"Politics!" interrupted Mr. Graeme, with some
warmth; "wha's fule eneugh to talk o' politics and
sic like clishmaclavers on a conveevial occasion. I
will hae Mr. Thompson and his wife in the bargain; they have aye been gude neeborly bodies, as
far as I ken to the contrairy, and his politics is
his ain business. I dinna care a bodle for Whig
or Tory; I'se warrant I hae them a' dancing the
reel o' Tullockgorum before the wee sma' hours the
night. And now I maun be ganging over to nee-
ber Alloway's, and hae a chat wi' that young Mr.
Carleton; he is a braw lad, and I hae taken a
prodigious fancy till him, not that I think ony
the less o' Maister Richard."

This last qualifying clause was intended as a
salve for Miss Lucy's feelings, whom he more than
suspected of nursing a strong partiality for the
cantie Laird of Woodbourne, and in whose ears his
praise of the captivating cavalier Carleton might
have an invidious bearing. But the conscious damsel, lilting forth a merry chorus, frisked away
beyond earshot ere he completed the sentence, and

left the good gentleman to chuckle over his threadbare joke as he ambled along the road to Woodbourne.

As we have intimated, the expected advent of
Mr. Waddell was looked forward to as an event of
uncommon interest,. inasmuch as his preaching there
would be the very first occasion that a minister
other than one of the Episcopal persuasion had
dispensed the bread of grace to perishing souls in
that vicinity. What gave it additional importance
was the fact that the rector of the parish, who
was a model of piety and good sense, then rarely
to be found among the regular custodians of the
public conscience in Virginia, had given formal
notice from the pulpit the Sunday before that, God
willing, the Rev. James Waddell, of the Hanover
Presbytery, would hold services in that church on
next Sabbath, and earnestly invoked the attendance
of the people on his brother's ministrations. The
announcement gave rise to considerable stir among
the more strait-laced members of the congregation,
especially when it was known that Parson Smith
had taken upon himself, without consulting the
wishes of the vestry, to tender the use of the
church to a person who had been denominated, in
the choice language of another clergyman, "a pick-
pocket, dark-lantern, moonlight preacher and enthusi-
ast," and ignominiously threatened with the whipping-
post if he persisted in his ministerial avocations. But
the general sentiment of the community warmly sup-
ported the liberal course of the minister in charge,
and there was no danger of Mr. Waddell's being sub-

12

jected to the shameful indignities he had met with a few years before in a neighboring parish.

Latterly, there has been considerable pother in certain quarters over the religious disturbances in Virginia during the colonial times. In the calm light of historical truth, they appear to be utterly insignificant, excepting in so far as they serve to throw light upon the condition of the Established Church, and upon the character and conduct of its ministry. They were a contemptible afterpiece, following the terrible drama of persecution in Europe.

There is no telling, to be sure, to what extent the mischief might have been carried had it not been for the discretion and forbearance which usually marked the deportment of the non-conforming ministers, and the wisdom and firmness of the measures which were taken by Governor Gooch to insure the observance of the Act of Toleration in its true spirit and intention. The established clergy, for the most part, clamorously asserted their claim to exclusive jurisdiction in ecclesiastical affairs, and strove in every way to nullify the operation of the law. The pope, says Selden, is infallible as long as he has the power to be obeyed. The parsons had no trouble in supporting their dangerous pretensions as long as they were aided and abetted by the civil authorities; but when that prop gave way, as was soon the case, the flimsy structure toppled to the ground never to rise again in its pristine proportions. No possible good can come of the attempt to revive the discussion of these discreditable proceedings, which have been made the handle of so much

unjust reproach and ungenerous criticism of the
Episcopal Church in Virginia. By common consent,
they are now ascribed by all fair-minded persons
to their real cause, which was found in the depravity
and weakness of many of those who wore the sacred
surplice, and who, in their daily walk and conversation, were anything else than examples of what
they were sent to preach. Looking back upon the
events of that stirring period, this feeble effort of
a handful of unpopular ecclesiastics to stem the
tide of free inquiry which was sweeping over the
land, excites in our breast only a passing emotion
of ridicule and contempt.

CHAPTER XII.

THAT is Clifton you see yonder," said Alloway to his friend, as they were riding over the farm, and having reached an elevated plateau near the river, had halted to enjoy the wide and delightful prospect which the spot afforded. Only a portion of the front of the house could be seen, but that was sufficient to give an adequate conception of the stateliness of the massive, reddish-brown edifice, which occupied the summit of the lofty promontory, formed by the confluence of the two main branches of the N—— river.

It is somewhat a fashion to speak of the bravest of the old colonial residences in Virginia as baronial—a term which is calculated by an obvious association of ideas to convey the impression of an imposing array of battlemented towers, frowning buttresses, and like insignia of feudal pomp and power. Assuredly the proud family seat of the Littleton's was as richly deserving of aristocratic designation as any quadrangular pile of imported bricks in the colony, both by reason of its intrinsic excellence, and of the dignity of its several owners. Still Clifton was by no means baronial in the sense in which the expression is ordinarily understood, having no sign nor token within or without of the lordly majesty which strikes terror to the soul of the beholder. True, the magnificent Lombardy poplars, ranged in a row and towering so straight and tall that their heads pierced the blue vault above them, might, to a romantic imagination, easily pass for so many faithful sentinels keeping watch and ward over the grisly stronghold of some uncouth giant; but, as the prosy fact was, they simply served the double purpose of decorating, with a tasteful display of exotic ornamentation, the curtilage of a substantial Virginian manor, and of furnishing a noted landmark for the pilots of the various crafts that plied up and down the Potomac. Its dimensions alone excepted, Clifton differed in nothing from its less pretentious and unbaronial neighbor, Bonhill, by which it was confronted from the opposite bank of the river.

The Littletons are a very ancient and eminently respectable family. No African explorer ever took greater pains to find the true sources of the "watery Nile" than we have done in trying to trace the lineage of the Littletons to its fountain head. Their antiquity has completely baffled our chronological investigations, and the reader must perforce be content with the traditionary assurance that our Littletons are genuine scions of the race which came out of one of the innumerable cells in the prolific hive of nations at a period the memory of man runneth not to the contrary, and that they became illustrious in more ways than one in the ups and downs, and ins and outs, of English history. This much may, however, be set down with positive cer-

12*

tainty as an episode which appropriately belongs to
our veracious chronicle. An ancestor of the Virginia Littletons was particularly distinguished for
his devotion to the royal cause in the great revolution, and was claimed to have been the sole,
ingenious contriver of the wonderful machinations
which afterwards enabled the fugitive son of the
unhappy martyr ·to elude the vigilance of his im·
placable pursuers. This infatuated "loyalist" fell
into the hands of the stern Protector, who grimly
nodded, and off went his head. But on the restoration of the monarchy, his son received the pos-
thumous recompense of loyalty in the shape of a
huge slice of the virgin soil of the Old Dominion.

A cool way that. Absolute Lord and Proprietary
Universal had of cutting "whangs out o' ither
folk's leather," as it no doubt appeared to the
untutored mind of Mr. Pope's poor Indian—

"Whose soul proud science never taught to stray
 Far as the solar walk or milky way,"

and who, for lack of astronomical knowledge, had for-
feited every right to terrestrial possessions. Possibly
he will be duly compensated in that "equal sky,"
to which he has been condescendingly admitted by
the gracious Muse. In this case, the grateful ben-
eficiary of royal munificence entered at once into
his vast territorial domain, and we do not learn
that there was ever a joinder on the mise to test
the validity of old Rowly's letters-patent.

In the after troubles which put an everlasting
quietus on the unfortunate house of Stuart, the
Virginia Littletons remained at heart faithful to

the cause of their benefactors, and being at a safe
distance from the theatre of strife, they were suffered to vent their loyal indignation without let or
hindrance, so long as they abstained from commit-
ting the overt act of treason against the reigning
dynasty. No friendly remonstrance was necessary,
it would seem, to keep them in the bounds of cautious circumspection. The bloody fate of their
unlucky ancestor was an efficient warning never
again to lose sight of the favorite Littleton maxim,
"*Nullum Numen abest, si sit Prudentia.*" And
whilst their lips overflowed with cheap professions
of unalterable attachment to their first and only
love, they took good care to withhold their contri-
bution of the material aid and comfort of purse
and sword, without which there was about as much
likelihood of the deposed Stuarts regaining their lost
crown as there is for any one of the present generation of American sovereigns to wield the sceptre
of the "coming empire."

This harmless zeal for a lost cause descended as
a muniment of title from father to son along with
the estate, and hence we find in the present pro-
prietor, Col. Robert Littleton, an uproarious Jaco-
bite in politics, and in religion, what was next of
kin to a papist, an inveterate highflyer, the proto-
type of the latter-day ritualist. With him the Stuart
mania was a sort of hereditary disease, which colored
and shaped every portent of the political heavens.
He was perpetually flying kites "over the river to
Charley," and it was the most provoking thing in
the world to him that all his neighbors did not
religiously believe with him, that the restoration of

his favorites would prove a panacea for every conceivable ill that could afflict the commonwealth of mankind. And he is far from being the only instance in history of such blind idolatry—such insane worship of graven images. At last, however, as we are credibly informed, he was entirely cured of his innate disorder. After the victory of Yorktown the conviction suddenly dawned upon him that the declaration of the United Colonies meant what it said—a plague on both your houses. Then the cherished vision melted into thin air; he submitted graciously to the irreversible decree, abandoned the land of his forefathers to its ignominious fate, joined heartily in the universal "all hail" to the rising star of the Western Hemisphere, and became in the end a blatant disciple of the most advanced school of progressive democracy. But we anticipate.

Notwithstanding his objectionable politics, Col. Robert Littleton was generally esteemed among his neighbors for possessing in a marked degree the amiable traits, rough and ready manners, and really hospitable disposition, which characterized his ideal standard of excellence in an opulent country gentleman, as he is portrayed to the life in Fielding's inimitable page. There was one insuperable obstacle in the way of Col. Littleton in his attempt to play the part of his illustrious pattern and exemplar with complete success. He had no foils to set off to advantage the salient points of imaginary resemblance. The estimable schoolmaster, who had taken his degrees at the University of Glasgow, and who was a Presbyterian of the straitest sect, had his

own orthodox notions concerning the unalterable
rule of right and the eternal fitness of things, and
these he inculcated, with equal impartiality and due
regard for the scriptural injunction, on the delicate sprigs of the house of Littleton and the
unkempt offspring of the commune pecus. And so
far from favoring the *soi-disant* squires' pretentions to
be considered the royal vice-gerent of the parish
in ecclesiastical matters, good Parson Smith never
once thought of consulting him in reference to the
text or duration of the hebdomadal discourse, nor
of inquiring into the nature of the dreams that
hovered above his cushioned dormitory in the
chancel. Yet he not only sent his sons regularly
every five days in the week to the old-field school,
which was presided over by the heretical Orbilius,
but maintained the most amicable relations with
the minister, paying his dues punctually in good
current tobacco, and quite satisfied with descanting
on the affairs of the Church at each stated vestry
meeting. For the rest, Squire Littleton, as he came
at last to be dubbed by the commonalty, dispensed
a generous hospitality in his own house, was no
laggard in partaking of the good cheer of his
neighbors, and bore his full share in every project
which was put forward to promote the general welfare of the community.

The master of Clifton is a widower, his wife
being dead years ago. His household is presided
over by Miss Theodora Littleton, who is so much
older than her brother that she may be said to
have reached the indefinable age at which the most
sanguine of superannuated maidens become reconciled

to the harsh allotment, which condemns them to
wither on the virgin thorn in unpitied desolation.
Of this pattern of spinsters, we have only one other
remark to make before she drifts out of sight like
a sobby log on the swift running stream of our
eventful story. She was, from all accounts, an
admirable housekeeper, considering that she never
had a house of her own to keep, swayed the rod
of domestic empire with a firm and even hand,
and devoted the hours she had to spare from the
cares of office to the ungrateful task of endeavor-
ing to inspire her willful niece with an apprecia-
tion of the tastes and fashions which obtained a
quarter of a century before the young lady was
born. To Miss Mary Littleton, "queen-rose of the
rose-bud garden of girls," our devoirs will be paid
in due season. The only other inmate of the mansion at present is the stranger guest, whose arrival
seems to have created no little commotion in the
usually quiet neighborhood. Col. Littleton has
another daughter, who is married, and lives in the
vicinity of Doughoregan Manor, in the Province of
Maryland, and two sons, who are off somewhere at
school.

During this interesting digression, Carleton has
had ample leisure for an exhaustive survey of the
premises. From looking at the old house, his eye
roves pleasantly over the fascinations of the surrounding scene. Presently he appears to be gazing
intently at some object on the water in front of
him. It was the veriest mite of a row-boat, which
a boy, with deft and graceful strokes, was making
to fly over the water with amazing rapidity.

"There goes your young sportsman, Dick," said he.

"Yes," replied Alloway, "that is Archie, with his inseparable rifle; but I was looking at that fellow yonder in the skiff—a sailor evidently. He must be one of the *Katrine's* crew; what can he want here?"

The man's appearance was eccentric, not to say suspicious. He was creeping cautiously along under the shadow of the boughs which overhung the stream, as if anxious to screen himself from observation, and was plainly watching the movements of the other little craft. While Alloway was speaking, the latter was headed for the landing at Clifton, seeing which, the man ran the skiff ashore, and, jumping out, disappeared in the wood.

"Deserted from his majesty's service afloat, is what that means, Dick," said Carleton.

"Very likely," replied Alloway. "Hallo, Harry, there they are," pointing, as he spoke, in the direction of Clifton.

A momentary glance revealed two figures on horseback—a lady and gentleman—as they dashed around the great circle in front of the house and disappeared in the mouth of the splendid avenue of native poplars and cedars, which conducted them out by the main entrance on the highway.

"My fair cousin, I am pleased to see," continued Mr. Richard, in a tone which was intended to convey the keenest irony and most superlative contempt, "has at last succeeded in finding a congenial companion in her equestrian excursions. She will not have a chance to decline the civility from me in a hurry, will she Don?" (patting the sympathizing sorrel caressingly on the neck). "Come, Harry, let us go."

Running his eyes again hurriedly over the surrounding scene, Carleton, gathering up the reins, turned and followed his companion.

"It is a humiliating confession, Dickon, my boy," said he, taking up the disagreeable topic. "The Chevalier Conrad has the inside track of us country bumpkins. Of course they will be of the party at Bonhill to-night?"

"Having been asked," replied Dick, mechanically, "I know of no reason why they should not go."

"Then," said Carleton, "I mean to tax my wits to the utmost but what I will learn all that is to be known about this gay prince Florizel, who comes masquerading here, to the dismay of the native chivalry."

"You can do as you like," replied Dick; "for my part, I wish Miss Littleton joy of her conquest, and hope she will have the good taste not to gratify your impertinent curiosity."

"Thank you kindly, my pink of good manners," said Carleton, acknowledging the civil speech with his best bow. "Then I am to expect neither help nor favor from you. *N'importe;* I'll wage the fight single-handed and alone, and the honor of the victory will be wholly mine. But why are you so venomously spiteful towards your cousin Mary? Everybody says she is very beautiful, and many sensible people have told me it was next to impossible to resist her fascinating ways."

Dick.—"Did you never see her?"

Harry.—"Yes; once when we were both mere children I remember going with my mother on a

visit to Clifton; she was then a little brown, hazel-
eyed chit in a pinafore and pantalettes, and, as I
thought, with a considerable touch of the tiger in
her composition. We had a pitched battle over my
whip-top, and she used her claws to such good purpose that my face and hands smart at the mention of it to this day. From which early experience
of her mettle, I would hazard the opinion that
Miss Littleton is, at all events, a decidedly plucky
girl in addition to her personal charms."

Dick (frowning majestically).—"She certainly does
not lack for beauty, and is, moreover, as they say,
very brilliant in conversation, manners, and all that;
nevertheless, I believe she is an artful, designing,
heartless coquette."

Harry.—"An artful, designing, heartless coquette!
You shock me beyond expression—

"'With every pleasing, every prudent part,
  Say, what does Chloe want? She wants a heart!'

A sad want truly. Who reigns o'er hearts, should
surely have a heart, and a big one at that. This
is a terrible accusation you bring against the 'famed
Belinda' of W——shire. Are you prepared with
the proofs? Where are the horrid witnesses of her
inhuman cruelty? Where the bleached bones of the
wretched victims whom this syren has lured to
their untimely doom? Come, I insist on your at
once producing the *corpus delicti*, as the lawyers
say, else the lady is acquitted, and you stand in
the pillory for rank perjury. What, dumb as an
oyster? It is then even as I conjectured—you can't
show so much as the metacarpal of a milk-sop
who has been brained with my lady's fan."

13

The whole of this humorous sally was lost on
Mr. Richard Alloway; he had, in the middle of it,
taken to whistling after his peculiarly dolorous
fashion, not indeed, like the love-lorn lout, for want
of thought, but as a running accompaniment to
certain unpleasant cogitations.

"Since she is disposed of," he said, musingly,
"I wonder who of the lovely dears will next set
up for a reigning belle on the stock-in-trade of
her ladyship's *lavings*, to borrow Mike's expression.
Mike was one day giving me a graphic description
of the heartless exactions of some of the landed
gentry in Ireland. 'Och, Misther Dick,' said he,
'they be like the *locusses* of Aigypt that Miss-
thress Murchieson (who is Mike's better half) was
rading to me about out of the Good Book; they
ates up everything as clane as the deck of a man-
o'-war, and gives the lavings to the poor.'"

Carleton laughed.

"Pray, who is this Mike I have heard you quote
so often?" he asked.

"Mike Burke," cried Alloway, seizing upon the
diverting theme with surprising avidity. "Is it possible I have never told you of my Milesian treasure, the most waggishly humorous and irresistibly
droll of the blundering tribe of St. Patrick. Let
me see, hang me, if I know much more of Mike's
juvenile days than I do of—,"

"The black-eyed troubador's," said Carleton smiling, as he pointed over his shoulder in the direction of Clifton.

"The devil," quoth Dick. "However, its of no
consequence; he was sufficiently well accredited when

he came here, and has since given hostages for his
future good behavior. It was I who got him his
wife. Mike, you must know, is a sailor, a genuine
old, weather-beaten son of Neptune, with a hand of
iron, and a heart—I was about to say of oak, but
I know it to be as soft as a woman's. There is
no place from China to Peru he has not visited;
he was with Captain Byron in his last cruise, and
sailed with Captain Cook in his first voyage around
the world; and you should hear him tell of the
wonders he saw 'ayont the antipodes.' But don't
intimate a doubt of his veracity if you value his
friendship. Well, he was picked up somewhere by
the skipper of the *Katrine*, with whom he made
one or two trips—I forget exactly how many—to
Virginia. In one of these flying visits he saw,
loved and courted in true sailor style, the buxom
widow Murchieson, whose late husband had been a
tenant of Mr. Graeme, and may be his Scotch red-
cousin in the eleventh degree. The widow liked
Mike well enough to marry him, but unluckily
she, in a gush of sorrowful good nature, promised
her deceased spouse that she would not take that
perilous leap in the dark a second time without
having obtained the consent and benison of Mr.
Graeme, and, for what reason I could never rightly
comprehend, the old gentleman positively forbade
the banns, or what amounted to the same thing,
he refused to have anything to do with the matter. Mrs. Murchieson, he said, was old enough to
choose a husband for herself, and he knew nothing
whatever, good or bad, of this wandering Jew of
an Irishman."

"I am sure that was reason a plenty for his refusal," suggested Carleton.

"For Mr. Graeme, yes; but it did not satisfy me. I had conceived a strong passion for Mike, and he was so bent on giving over his nomadic, sea-faring life, and spending the rest of his days in peace and quiet under the widow's tempting vine and fig tree, that I got his captain to go with me to see Mr. Graeme and intercede in his behalf. After considerable persuasion on our part, and an earnest appeal from Miss Lucy, he at length relented and signed the paper I had prepared, saying, as he did so, in his cautious manner: 'Weel, weel, lads, Dame Murchieson maun gang her ain gate, that is, wi' my permission, and gin she finds to her dool she has forgathered wi' a beggar, she maun mak' the maist o' a bad bargain; she kens the proverb well enough.' Mike was happy, so was the widow, and from that day we have been fast friends. But I have never been able to correct one bad habit in Mike. He will persist in calling Mr. Graeme 'yer riverence.' Doubtless he intends thereby the highest possible respect; but the worthy gentleman does not like the idea of being taken for a papist priest, although he has not the holy horror of popery that some people profess."

Harry.—"How has your interesting old sea-dog fared ashore?"

Dick.—"Oh, he is a very model of hen-pecked Benedicts. Like a good many others who have weathered that Cape of Good Hope, he found the land he had reached was far from being the 'cloudless Olympus' of a lover's fancy. Mrs. Murchieson,

as he still calls his wife, has her little pilfering
tempers, and when thoroughly roused, her. wrath,
says Mike, is tenfold worse than the raging sea.
But he has his boat, and the friendly river runs
close by their cabin, and as soon as a speck of
cloud rises on the domestic horizon, he rushes
headlong for the beach and puts to sea, no matter
for the weather, until the storm ashore has subsided. He informed me once, as a great secret,
that he never stood in so much awe of but one other
being, which was the 'Admiral,' as he calls Captain
Cook, and surely if rank and merit went always
hand in hand, no man in his majesty's navy better
deserves the title. It mattered not how hard the
wind blew, if the captain was in a fret, the cross-
trees, said Mike, was a more comfortable berth
than the quarter-deck. The piping of old Boreas
in his most frantic mood was delightful music in
comparison with the terrible clangor of the speaking
trumpet in the hands of this born ruler of the
roughest of his race. But it is impossible for me
to do justice to Mike's hero. Have you read the
account of his marvellous voyage?"

Harry.—"Only such snatches of it as have appeared in the public prints."

Dick.—"Then I have a rare entertainment in
store for you. What say you to a sail in Mike's
fishing smack, and a thrilling chapter or so from
his inexhaustible log-book?"

Harry.—"I should like it of all things, next to
a cruise with the great 'Admiral' himself. I agree
with you in your estimate of Cook's abilities. He
has not only proved himself to be the most daring

13*

and skillful navigator of the day, but he has also
evinced the highest qualities of a great naval commander. I wish we had a dozen like him in command of as many good, stout ships of war, we
would soon teach the insolent, self-styled mistress
of the seas that she has no charter to ravage and
despoil at will, merely to make good the prophetic
anthem of her guardian angels, 'Britons shall
never be made slaves!' For was it not so written
in the book of destiny, says or sings the mighty
bard—

> "'When Britain first at heaven's command,
> Arose from out the azure main?'

And this gasconading twaddle was actually rewarded
with the guerdon of a sycophant's ambition, a sin-
ecure office under government! Slaves, did he say?
What has he done with the angelic creatures, who
were auctioned off at Rome to the highest bidder?"

"Those were unfortunate captives, Harry," said
Dick, vainly trying to rescue the "free-born Britons" from a merciless belaboring. "Part of the
spolia opima of the Roman conqueror."

"No such thing," continued Carleton, giving the
reins to his hobby-horse. "Either history is a
colossal lie, or these same thrasonical braggarts were
little better than a nation of slaves from the day
that Cæsar planted his standard on their sacred
soil to that on which the Norman despot's iron heel
stamped out the last lingering spark of liberty, and
they remained for centuries the pusillanimous serfs
and villains of feudal tyranny. Besides, they have
meekly endured every phase of anarchy and revolution, passed through the flames of religious per-

secution, and suffered all the calamities of lawless usurpation and grinding oppression. And even now they are the obedient, submissive vassals of the vile tyrant, who seeks to bind us with galling chains."

"Breathe awhile, Harry," said Dick, "and at 'em again. Your invective is superb. What does Addison say? Oh, I have it:

"'Tis liberty that crowns Brittania's isle,
And makes her barren rocks and her bleak mountains smile.'

Was I ranting in good earnest, Dick?" inquired his companion, with an innocent look. "Oh, how I do detest the trumpery fustian stuff called eloquence—all sound and fury, signifying nothing. It was Cortez, I believe, who said that some things should be done before they were thought upon—a proper maxim for a foolhardy, hair-brained adventurer. Yet certain it is, that over-much talking about a matter of life and death importance is apt to beget irresolution and fatal delay in its execution. Many a flighty purpose has gone careering to the limbo of vanity on the furious gale of windy declamation. Has not Patrick Henry said all that can be said on the subject? Then why do not our conscript Fathers declare at once for independence, and cease to talk about it?"

"It will require a legion of light-horse to back the declaration, brave captain," said Dick.

"Yes," replied the impetuous Carleton; "and they can be had at a minute's warning. Every man in Virginia will leap to arms at the first note of that inspiring tocsin."

There was nothing in this eager outburst incon-
sistent with his previous utterances. He saw that
the conflict was inevitable; he anticipated the final
result, and his soul was filled with the sublime
thought of a young nation liberated from colonial
bondage, and starting upon its career of imperishable glory.

At this stage of the conversation, our cavaliers
were interrupted by a messenger, who came to say
that Mr. Graeme awaited their presence at the
house, and glad to escape from their dangerous
society, we will invite the reader to continue his
round of junketting in more agreeable company.

CHAPTER XIII.

THE lady and gentleman whose appearance gave rise to the foregoing animadversions of Mr. Richard Alloway, in a little while have returned from their morning jaunt on horseback. But it is all too charming—the luxurious effulgence of the glorious autumnal sky—to be imprisoned within doors, and they have barely entered the house before they come forth again, this time equipped for a walk. After a turn or two on the spacious terrace, and around the grand circle, and down the broad avenue, they are finally discovered idly wandering through the groves and glades of the deerless park which skirts the lawn on the side nearest to the river. A gigantic oak has been blown down in a furious gale last summer. It is clinging desperately to life by one frail root, and its proud head, now a shapeless mass of ruin, hangs helplessly over a dismal hollow. To the moralist it presented the familiar symbol of dethroned majesty—of the sure fate that overtakes alike the loftiest and lowliest of mortal men. Otherwise rugged and forlorn, to say nothing of its proximity to the deep and dark ravine, the spot had none of the attractive features of the poetical trysting-place of "Love's young dream." Yet here the ramblers pause; the gentleman assists the lady to a seat on the gnarled trunk of the prostrate giant, and himself leans gracefully against a shattered limb.

In one respect, Mr. Richard Alloway's portrait of his fair cousin has not exceeded the bounds of truthful delineation. It is the most bewitchingly beautiful face in the world that is looking up at its companion out of a wondrous glory of clustering brown curls, and it is moreover apparent to a connoisseur in such matters that the deep, earnest, adoring expression of those eloquent eyes could not possibly be counterfeited by the most consummately wicked of coquettes. There is no denying the soft impeachment—

> Love in her sunny eyes doth basking play,
>   Love walks the pleasant mazes of her hair,
> Love does on both her lips forever stray,
>   And sows and reaps a thousand kisses there.

And in her case, these outward and visible tokens of an inward and spiritual grace plainly denoted that love had gone within, and nestled like a dove in the warmest corner of her heart.

But, out upon the "rude Carinthian boor" of a limner, who has done the handsome and houseless stranger such unmannerly despite. True, his abundant and flowing tresses, worn in contempt of the prevailing mode, are the hue of the raven's wing, but they shade a brow and features that are strikingly noble, intelligent and attractive, and

so far from wearing a ferocious or even austere
aspect, the full, black orbs have quenched their
fiery darts in a flood of tenderest lustre, and repay
the lady her loving gaze with usury. He is speaking, and although his language is English, pure
and fluent, he makes no attempt to disguise the
marked accent which betrays his foreign nativity.

"There is no longer room for a reasonable doubt
on the subject," said he, pursuing a theme in
which he was intensely interested. "Your late
cousin, Mr. Richard Austin, answers perfectly to
the description of our incognito. No wonder the
Abbé's usual penetration failed him here—he had
no earthly ground to suspect that the object of
his search was all that time hiding from his most
intimate friends. It was his nephew, you tell me,
with whom I had the pleasant encounter of the
fox hunt? I should not have divined the relation-
ship from any external resemblance to the original
of the picture, as drawn by the master of the
Grande Chartreuse—the one a frail, delicate, pale-
eyed, silver-toned and morbidly sensitive student;
the other, a stout, hirsute, bold and devil-may-care
sportsman, with the brawn of a Milo, and the lungs
of a Stentor."

The lady smiled.

"It would, indeed, be difficult," she replied, "to
find two near kinsmen more utterly dissimilar in
personal appearance. But you wrong my cousin
Richard if you imagine he is only the stature,
bulk, and big assemblance of a man. He is a
noble-hearted, brave and generous fellow, if he has
of late taken up a most unaccountable dislike of
me."

"And thereby established his claim to my regard," said Conrad, laughingly. "I readily forgive him his making merry over my ridiculous misadventure; it served me right for coming in at the fag end of the chase to try to rob him of his well-earned laurels. But his behavior in the other case—"

"Nay," cried Miss Littleton, in the same bantering tone, "I reject your championship. Leave me to fight my own battles with this great giant, and you will, in no time, behold a bloodless triumph, no love lost, and no bones broken. After all, it was a trifling matter to quarrel about, and if he is as heartily ashamed of it as I am, there will be no trouble in bringing about a speedy restoration of our former amicable relations. On due reflection, I am convinced that I was the party most at fault. There can be no excuse for the rude and scornful manner in which I repudiated his well-meant intercession in a dear friend's behalf. A woman is apt to exaggerate offences when she is conscious of imprudence in giving occasion for invidious criticism. I remember being exceedingly indignant with him at the time, and I did not scruple to berate him soundly for having been the cause of a painful misunderstanding with the Graemes, to whom I was really attached."

"Did he accuse you flatly of having jilted Mr. George Graeme?" asked Conrad.

"Yes," replied Mary, "or at least his language implied as much, and besides, he called me a little fury, and, I verily believe, he wished I had been a man, that he might take me to personal account. To be sure, he apologized for his angry conduct, but I was so much incensed at the thought of a rupture with my friends at Bonhill, the result of his awkward intermeddling, that I repulsed his overtures, and thus the matter stands open between us at present. Unfortunately for me, the reputed victim of my artful wiles was gone away to Scotland, and so Dame Gossip had everything her own way. But worst affliction, I had to endure my good aunt's interminable lectures; for, strange to say, she obstinately refused to listen to one word of explanation from me, and charged my delinquencies, as she was pleased to call them, to the account of setting at naught her wholesome admonitions. In such a desperate strait, there was no recourse left me but to fly for shelter to my sister in Maryland."

"In which hegira from persecution, you have furnished another striking illustration of the proverb which has been so often exemplified in my humble career, '*L'Homme propose et Dieu dispose*,'" exclaimed the passionate lover.

"Take care how you bless your stars on the event," replied the wayward damsel, with a saucy glance, "for, if report be true, you have this time experienced the truth of a different adage altogether, and only caught a Tartar for your pains. There, let go my hand and behave like a rational being. And, since you are in the sentimental vein, tell me a pretty love story out of your book of romantic chronicles, and, in return, I will improvise you an Indian legend."

"Another time, under favor, my gracious queen," said Conrad. "You forget I have an appointment

14

with the Abbé, which I must on no account fail
to keep."

"It had indeed escaped me," replied Mary, looking grave. "Are you compelled to go this afternoon?"

Conrad.—"I am; the business between us admits
of no delay."

Mary.—"How very provoking. I had set my
heart on your going to Bonhill to-night, and being
introduced to the company by your proper name
and title."

Conrad.—"I fear you will be deprived of that
gratification. What is the distance to Yeocomico,
the place at which I am to meet the Abbé?"

Mary.—"Scarcely an hour's ride. What is that
noise?"

There was a strange rustling sound among the
leaves of the fallen oak, although there was not a
breath of wind astir.

"Only a bird," said Conrad, replying to her
look of alarm.

The explanation was plausible, but it did not
allay Miss Littleton's suspicions. As the conversation proceeded, she was repeatedly observed to cast
uneasy glances in the direction whence the sound
proceeded.

"Suppose now," she went on to say, "that I
were to insist upon your deferring this visit until
to morrow morning?"

"*Pardonnez-moi, ma belle amie,*" replied her companion; "but it is not a supposable matter. You
are aware that the ship is ready to put to sea
with the first favorable gale after midnight, and I

am no more a Prospero than you are a Lapland
witch or other kind of contraband dealer in contrary winds. Besides, the excellent father makes
free use of the imperative mood in his missive,
and we have a great many things to talk over.
Of course I shall be required to answer for my
dealings with a certain incorrigible little heretic,
and what have I to urge in my defence? Absolutely nothing. Only a miracle of grace can save
me from the awful expiation of an *auto-da-fè*. The
Abbé is a master of the art of persuasion, but
even his eloquence would be lost on such an ob-
stinate rebel. Convert her! He may as well go
with good St. Anthony and preach salvation to
the fishes."

At this audacious speech the young lady bridled
up with the best imitation of offended dignity she
could muster on so short a notice. There was one
subject on which these lovers had very prudently
resolved mutually to exercise the largest amount of
the liberty of liberties—*videlicet*—the liberty of dis-
agreeing. In the archest manner imaginable, and
with the aptest exhibition of ironical humor, she
held up a taper finger, on which glittered a ring
begemmed with costly jewels.

"Since it is to the confessional you are going,
my poor penitent," said she with mock compassion, "be sure you carry the sin-offering with
you;" then suddenly pouting and affecting the air
and tone of injured beauty, which has a right to
be absurdly jealous and outrageously exacting, she
added lachrymosely, "I believe you love Father
Soulé better than you do anybody else in the
world."

"Not exactly," said Conrad, earnestly. "But it is quite probable I should have been unworthy of the love of *one* body in the world had it not been my good fortune to have for a mentor, at once the best, the gentlest and the wisest of men. You should have heard what Mr. Carroll said of him if you deem my encomium extravagant. 'Father Soulé,' he said to me one day, in his deliberate manner, 'approaches, in my estimation, as near to being a pure and perfect intelligence as it is possible to conceive of in a finite and fallible mortal.' His learning is only excelled by his piety, and both are unfathomable. He is a philosopher without scepticism, a polemic without acerbity, a priest without bigotry. The most subtle and profound of thinkers, the most captivating of reasoners, the most erudite of scholars, the humblest of believers, he is what Socrates might have been had he too been a Christian."

"A wonderful character, truly, for a Jesuit priest," exclaimed the persistent heretic, "for such I understand is your incomparable guide, philosopher and friend."

Conrad was now constrained to take up the cudgels for his tutor in downright earnest. "Yes," said he, "I do not blush to proclaim it in spite of the late extraordinary decree of Rome. He does belong to that illustrious society which has been so grievously scandalized by the conduct of unworthy members, and his life has been a shining example of its sublime motto—All things for the greater glory of God."

"And pray tell me," retorted the fair disputant,

"whence came the prerogative of your magnificent order to that pious posy? To my thinking, it is of the essence of religion the world over to ascribe all honor, praise and glory to Him from whom cometh every good and perfect gift. It is certainly so taught in my Bible and Prayer Book. All things for the greater glory of God? Why it is the soul of Christian worship, the burden of every sacred missal, the universal doxology of devotional piety, and you would appropriate it to adorn the phylactery of an effete monkish institution. That will do, not another syllable, as you are a gallant gentleman; I claim the privilege of my sex, the last word. You began the dispute without warning, I will put an end to it with equal abruptness. You have neglected to say whether or not my poor cousin's death necessitates an alteration in your plans."

"That will be as the good father will decide," replied Conrad, now all meek submission.

"And has not the good father's dutiful son any opinion of his own on so vital a subject?"

"*He-bien!* It is really my poor opinion to which your ladyship attaches so great value." Then growing suddenly serious, he proceeded. "The plan of procedure shall not be changed in a single particular with my consent. The proofs, to be sure, are not sufficient in law; there is one link missing in the chain of evidence which only Mr. Austin could have supplied. But I am not a suppliant of British justice. I expect no redress at the hands of my father's malignant enemies; my lot in that regard is now irrevocably fixed; henceforth, for

14*

weal or woe, I am an American. My private score with a sworn and implacable foe shall not turn me from the line of duty; he may procrastinate the day of settlement, but as a just God reigneth, he will live to see the consequences of his unnatural guilt. To-morrow your father shall know my whole history, from which time I shall assume my rightful name, rank and station."

"Why not allow me the privilege of telling it all to my friends this very night?" eagerly inquired Mary Littleton.

"So be it," replied Conrad, after a moment's reflection. "Provided, of course, that I get back in time to bear you company. Still it is proper for me to inform Colonel Littleton who I am, and to learn what he has to say about the after introduction. You must remember, too, there is another important matter about which he is to be consulted."

The lady looked up inquiringly, but there was no need of explanation; the rosy flush which suffused her cheek showed how truly she interpreted his meaning glance.

"Does Father Soulé approve your sending this letter to the person they call Sir William Markham?" she asked, covering her momentary confusion by recurrence to the previous engrossing topic.

"More than that," replied Conrad; "the letter was originally written at his dictation two months ago. I could not trust myself to phrase it after what had occurred between us." His thin lips grew tremulous with suppressed passion, and a sudden gleam like lightning from a passing summer cloud shot from the speaker's brilliant eyes. "The bloody reckoning was not of my seeking; my mission to England was for peace and reconciliation, to heal the gaping wounds which civil broils had made in our unhappy house, and I was ready to make every sacrifice but *one* to secure that consummation. Even now, my terms are fair, honorable and just. If Sir William Markham again rejects them, on his head shall rest the guilt of keeping open wounds that may rankle to the death."

The vehemence of his manner, and his lofty mien, elate and instinct with conscious power to will and to do, brought a bright glow of admiration to the lovely features of his companion; but before she could frame a reply, the limbs of the great oak were violently shaken, which startling phenomenon was immediately followed by a dull thud and the crackling sound of breaking twigs, as though some heavy body had fallen to the ground and rolled down the side of the ravine. Conrad ran to the edge and peered over. Then, with a loud shout, he bounded down the bank in pursuit, as fast as the dense thicket of undergrowth permitted. Presently he came panting back, with a small sporting rifle in his hand.

"The scamp was too fleet for me," he said; "but he has lost his gun."

"It is Archie's," replied Mary, "and here he is. What is the matter child? The gentleman will not harm you."

The question did not imply alarm; for barring a

scratch on the cheek, the lad was not hurt, and his buckskin hunting suit was briar and bramble proof; but his face showed signs of deep vexation and shame.

"I'm not afraid of him," he said, his color deepening as he shot a fiery glance at Conrad, who was regarding him with a half amused, half-admiring look. "Indeed, Miss Mary, it was an accident my being here. I saw you coming, and hid in the tree for fun."

"Queer notion of fun, you little eavesdropper," said Conrad.

Again the boy's face grew crimson with indignation, and his eyes flashed defiance at his accuser.

"It is false," he cried. "Miss Mary, you—,"

"Do not believe you capable of such an act, Archie," replied the lady, hastening to his relief; "nor shall this gentleman do you such injustice in his thoughts, if I can help it. Mr. Conrad, this is the little friend of whom you have heard me speak."

"And whose acquaintance I have so much desired to make," said Conrad, with winning courtesy; "I recall the offensive expression; there, my little fellow, take your pretty gun, and with it my hand, and thus, there is an end of it. Now, hie away after that 'bunny" that's chattering down there in the ravine, and leave Miss Littleton and me to finish our conversation."

"Stay, Archie," exclaimed Mary, as the boy turned to go; "who is that man?"

Conrad and the boy looked quickly in the direction she pointed, and saw a man dressed in the garb

of a sailor, some fifty paces distant, walking hurriedly through the Park towards the river. Another
moment he was out of sight.

"It isn't Mike," said Archie; "I'll run after him
and see—,"

"No, no," said Mary, hastily; "it does not matter. Go on to the house and tell aunt Mr Conrad
is going away before dinner, and don't go home
until I see you again; I have something to send
your mother. That's a good boy; there's a kiss
for you."

Archie blushed in acknowledgment of the favor,
and, bowing gracefully to Conrad, scampered off as
she requested.

"Your page is very obedient, but why so thoughtful, lady mine?" said Conrad, observing that the
capricious damsel was following the boy with a
serious gaze. Mary started, blushing slightly.

"It is nothing," she said, "only a foolish fancy;"
but seeing that he still regarded her with a questioning look, she proceeded: "You remember as we
were riding home this morning through the wood,
we heard the report of a gun. It caused me to
turn my head, and, fast as we were going, I caught
sight of that same man skulking among the bushes
near the road. He was looking straight at me, and
a more forbidding face, though I saw it for an
instant only, I never looked on. When I discovered him just now he was peering at Archie from
behind that tree in a stealthy manner. At once a
suspicion took hold of me that he was dogging
the boy's steps for some evil purpose. Quite absurd, wasn't it?"

"By no means," said Conrad; "the suspicion was natural enough. What a spitfire the lad is; it is well for me he was disarmed. I like his spirit."

Mary.—"And if he were eavesdropping, it is precious little he got for his trouble."

Conrad.—"True; what a model pair of turtle doves we are to be sure."

Lovers have an incomprehensible language for which there is neither lexicon nor grammar. Why the other "dove" should spring from her perch and dart like an arrow so quickly across the glade at that innocent allusion, was to the uninitiated observer an unaccountably strange proceeding. Away she sped through the park, nor paused in her flight until she reached the open lawn and caught sight of Aunt Theodora's vigilant face looking out at her chamber window. Then she turned upon her baffled pursuer with a silvery peal of defiance, to which the discomfited swain replied with the baldest pretence of supreme nonchalance.

Passing the reviewing officer with the most precise decorum, the lovers entered the house.

"Now," said Mary, "I must go and have a lunch got ready for you while you are making preparations for your ride."

Conrad's rapturous gaze followed her graceful form as she tripped away on her errand. "Behold!" he exclaimed, in a transport of feeling, "the first gift of my adopted land—a treasure I would not barter for all the wealth and dignities that kings can bestow. The Abbé must surely approve my choice, unless he intends I shall never marry.

How unlucky he should be called away so suddenly. At least we must contrive to detain this vessel, if only for a day. He will then have an opportunity of seeing her before he goes on this perilous voyage." So saying, he hastened to get ready for his journey.

CHAPTER XIV.

IT is the night of the party. Bonhill is aglow with a blaze of glory, and flames afar like a cheering beacon from its hill of pride. Cavalcade after cavalcade of country beaux and belles are pouring in, and soon the jocund sounds of revelry are floating gaily on the palpitating air. Old Uncle Phil, the black fiddler, like another Timotheus, or ebony image of the musical god himself, raised on high, rules the monarch of a season over as goodly a company of fair women and brave men as ever moved submissive to the spell of enchanting minstrelsy. *Chacun a son gout.* Let such as like, "dance after a Monsieur's flageolet," or, if they prefer, "have a set of English viols to their concert;" but for the kind of melody which puts life and mettle into heel and toe, which "awakes the pert and nimble spirit of mirth and turns melancholy forth to funerals," there is no instrument of music which bears comparison with a tuneful fiddle under the skillful manipulation of some sable Orpheus from Old Virginia's shore. O, the wonderful works of nature! Who would imagine that the soul of harmony resided in the entrails of a caterwauling grimalkin? How the secret was first made known is a question about which there is much diversity of opinion among learned Thebans, so we will cut the matter short by agreeing with the "auld gabbit poets," that

> Jove's nimble son and leckie snel
> Made the first fiddle of a shell,
>   On which Apollo,
> With mickle pleasure, played himsel
>   Baith jig and solo.

It is the first time that Bonhill has witnessed such a scene of merriment and glee; but not the last by a countless number. Ofttimes have we beheld the like display in those cheery old halls—little or nothing changed, save in the names and costumes of the actors; danced the same minuets and country dances, reels and rigadoons, and cut nameless fantastic capers to the lively strains of the identical cremona bequeathed from sooty sire to son; listened to the like merry din of inarticulate voices and clatter of many twinkling feet; the same gladsome chimes of silvery laughter, rustling of silken folds, and, crowning all, the deft prompter's gutteral tones calling out the figures of the dance—every charming feature as fresh and joyous as on that first night when youth and pleasure here forgathered "to chase the glowing hours with flying feet."

There is no observance here of formal ceremony, and staid etiquette; all things are conducted on

15

that indescribably free and easy plan and decorous
regard of unstudied politeness which was the ruling
trait of the social gatherings of the olden time in
Virginia. The guests are, for the most part, known
to each other, and the unacquainted are soon relieved of embarrassment by a general introduction.

The first dance is ended; some of the company
are promenading in couples, others enjoying a quiet
tête-à-tête in a cozy corner, and, here and there, a
little group appears to be drawn together by the
magnetism of some acknowledged belle. In the
centre of one of these charmed circles shines re-
splendent the beautiful star of Clifton. Her coming unattended by the strange gentleman was the
occasion of much surprise and some disappointment.
The explanation she vouchsafed of his absence only
served to enhance the general interest, and she was
made to run the gauntlet of inquisitive tongues.
Having borne the infliction for some time with
commendable suavity and good humor, she at length
seeks refuge from her tormentors by engaging in a
keen encounter of wit and raillery with a sprightly
young gentleman, who has only the day before
arrived home from a long sojourn abroad. This is
Mr. Charles Copland, Jr., late student of law of
Grey's Inn, London, where he has performed the
customary gastronomical exercises with more than
ordinary credit. Though she sustains her part in
the conversation with considerable spirit and vivacity,
it is evident on narrower scrutiny that her thoughts
are far from being wholly engrossed thereby. Occa-
sionally her shafts fly at random, and once in a
while she is detected shooting a furtive glance

across the room where Carleton is observed talking
to Lucy Graeme in a sedate and earnest manner,
which is strangely at variance with the prevailing
gaiety.

That arch diplomatist has lost no time in laying
his wily toils. Conscious of the delicacy of the
undertaking, he had set about it with an adroit-
ness which would have done credit to the genius
of a Temple or a Walsingham. While the dance
was going on he found a ready pretext for broach-
ing the entertaining subject of his recent explora-
tions to his partner, and so managed that Miss
Littleton should hear such significant snatches of
the story as to awaken her suspicions and arouse
an eager desire to hear the whole of it. Now, it
so happened that the object of his artful scheming
was at the same time revolving in her mind how
she could contrive to obtain certain information
from Mr. Richard Alloway of the supposed mysterious adventures of his late uncle while in Europe,
and the apparently casual remarks which reached
her ears in the rounds of the dance satisfied her
that Carleton was in possession of the matter she
sought to discover.

Our friend Dick, we blush to record, was so un-
gracious as to decline to meet his fair cousin's
advances towards reconciliation at the half-way house
of mutual concession; he was inflexibly offish, stiff
and punctilious in his demeanor towards her. With
Lucy it was *tout au contraire*, not a word was
spoken of the disagreeable past; they glided at
once into their former intimate relations and were
the Rosalind and Celia of old, forgetful that a

single cloud had ever darkened the heaven of re-
ciprocal regard and congenial attachment. Presently,
Carleton joins the group who are gathered around
Mary Littleton, and claims her hand for the next
dance.

"Would you believe it, Mr. Carleton," she exclaimed, after acknowledging his demand, "here is
a gentleman all the way from London by the last
packet who cannot, for his life, tell a body a word
about the latest vogues? His talk is of nothing
but the long-winded debates in Parliament, the
grand sights he saw at my Lord Mayor's show, the
ghostly mementoes of Westminster Abbey, the monu-
mental mockeries of the hideous old Tower, and I
don't know how many other equally dull and stupid
things which we untraveled ignoramuses, of course,
never heard or read of before, and here I am
dying to learn if my *aigrette* is *à-la-mode*, my hair
properly craped, my tucker such as ladies of quality
wear, whether, in a word, I be *poin'-devise* in all
all my accoutrements."

"I am glad you have come to my rescue, Carleton," meekly responded the crest-fallen limb of the
law. "You see now what a fellow gets for being
so deucedly patriotic. I heartily wish I had stayed
in London after what I have gone through since
my return. What a dolt I was to entertain so
absurd a delusion. Just imagine my thinking all
this long while that my fair country-women were
ever so busy, like true Spartan maids and matrons,
setting the example of independence—clothing themselves in the products of their own industrious
looms and spindles, knitting stockings for General

Washington's soldiers, and doing all manner of self-sacrificing things, and just look at them, tricked out in all their finery, chattering about the latest fashions from London and Paris, and denying me the welcome they would readily bestow on any smuggling pedler of new-fangled haberdashery. Beauty when unadorned, adorned the most! Sentimental stuff! Why, what would a woman be without the—,"

Carleton, ever ready, comes to his assistance with a handy tag of rhyme:

> "The powder, patches, and the pins,
> The ribbons, jewels and the rings,
> The lace, the paint and warlike things
> That make up all their magazines?"

"Thank you, Harry."

"Cowley, you mean; the words are not mine," replied the artful chevalier, with an apologetic bow to the ladies.

"Never mind," retorted Copland, "I am not afraid to adopt the quotation, if you are. Why, even Bella yonder—bless her little heart, how she cried when her big brother was sent away and there was no one to play with her—even Bella, I say, now a woman grown, wept bitter tears of anguish in secret when she heard that I had not brought her a new silk gown. Well, there is nothing for me to do but to swallow my mortification with the best grace possible. At least there is a grain of consolation in the loss of your kind favor, ladies, in the consciousness of having duly respected the laws of my country. My entire invoice of imported articles is summed up in a new book of songs for Miss Lucy, and Scotch high-dried enough to keep my respected father sneezing through a year's siege."

"Pray, tell me, Mr. Censor," said Mary, in the same bantering tone, "what is the harm of our wearing fine clothes, if we happen to have them? Then, sir, you forget that the prohibition is against English goods. You might have bought Bella's gown in Paris, where, I dare say, you spent the worth of a dozen frolicking and sight-seeing with that rantipole cousin of mine, Frank Tunstall, as you told us awhile ago."

"Frank Tunstall! Did he return with you?" asked Carleton.

"No," said Copland; "when I parted from him in Paris he was preparing to set out on the grand tour. Frank is become to be very much a citizen of the world."

"And a greater coxcomb than ever, I imagine?" said Carleton.

"Well, yes," replied Copland; "he has cultivated fashionable fopperies at a prodigious rate; yet, with all his dandified airs and priggish notions, he is by no means such a vapid creature as you think—at least, he is not deficient in spirit. By the way, Miss Mary, I did not tell you how we both came to be in Paris. Well, as I said, Frank's ruling pas-sion is to be a fine gentleman, and being hand-some and rich, and well-bred and all that, he soon got the entrée of the *beau monde*, where he sported like a gorgeous butterfly. Could you hear him descant on their daily rounds, you would not won-der that our dear cousins have no time to attend to the humble petitions with which we, as in duty bound, have been clamorously besieging the throne of kingly grace; they are literally overwhelmed with the grievous cares of their unhappy state which condemns them to oscillate eternally between the extremes of ennui and dissipation. Frank deemed this exquisite mode of killing time to be the acme of refined beatitude, and he was was never a Sabbath day's journey from his darling London, until an unlucky contretemps fell out—,"

"A love scrape with a maid of honor?" said Mary Littleton.

"Pinkèd a young sprig of nobility in a duel?" said Carleton.

"Neither," replied Copland; "though quite as bad as the one or the other. Returning home one night from the opera, he took it into his head to venture alone into White's, that paradise of *beaux garçons* and *hommes de condition*—anglice fashionable rakes and genteel sharpers—where, not content with the innocent diversion of being plucked for a docile pigeon, he very foolishly suffered himself to be inveigled into talking of politics. Of course, in such a select assembly of loyal blades, the rabble rout of American rebels were denounced, as they should be, and the rash, intruding Virginian was not long in finding himself an unwilling auditor of all manner of scurrilous allusions, objurgations and sneers, poured out without stint or measure on his countrymen. He managed to keep his choler down and sustain the unequal combat of billingsgate and bravado until one of his assailants made some disparaging speech about General

Washington, who, among other claims to distinction, has the honor to be nearly related to Frank on his mother's side. A knock down, a general scuffle and uproar, and all is dark to our hero until he awakes next morning with a dim and confused perception of what had happened, and a humiliating conviction that he was certainly demented to venture by himself in that den full of the British lion's whelps. He was lucky to get off with only a bruised lip and one eye in mourning; but such was his mortification that I had no trouble in persuading him to pack his portmanteau and take the first diligence for Dover. In a fortnight's time I joined him in Paris, where I found him revelling in the elysian delights of the gay metropolis and railing in bad French at everything English in a way that made the natives stare."

"And when is the splendid creature coming back to the land of savages?" asked Mary.

"In the spring, he said," replied Copland. "I shall promise him, when I write, a perfect ovation from *les belles-sauvages!*"

The young lawyer was in rapid retreat when he discharged this Parthian arrow. As soon as he was gone the little coterie dispersed, and Carleton and Miss Littleton fell into line with the promenaders.

The diplomatist begins: "Miss Graeme tells me she expected a rare addition to her company this evening. She seems much disappointed that he did not come; to be frank, so am I."

"Indeed?"

"Yes; the gentleman to whom I allude is Mr. Conrad."

"Oh, my father's guest. I have already endured a siege of questioning on account of his failure to put in an appearance here to-night. Pray, why are you so deeply concerned about it?"

"From a better motive, I beg you will believe, than impertinent curiosity. I have an important reason for desiring to make Mr. Conrad's acquaintance. I am very much exercised over an investigation of certain transactions of your late cousin, Mr. Richard Austin, while traveling in Europe many years ago, and I have a notion that Mr. Conrad can be of service to me in the matter."

Mary was visibly disconcerted by the grave and business-like precision with which he opened the conversation. She regarded him with a look of puzzled surprise.

"Is it a confidential secret, Mr. Carleton?" she ventured timidly to ask. "In your turn, you have said enough to stimulate my curiosity, of which eminently feminine weakness I profess to have my full share."

A preliminary scraping of the fiddle interrupted Carleton's reply.

"The music is about to begin," he said; "we must take our places for the dance."

"Are you fond of dancing, Mr. Carleton?" asked Mary.

"Y-es, with a pleasant partner; usually, though, I more enjoy looking on at others."

"Then, suppose you play spectator this time, and continue the conversation you have started."

"I am delighted you have made the proposition."

"Where are you going, Harry?" cried Dick Allo-

way, as they moved aside to make room for the
dancers. "You are wanted here to make up the
set."

"Please, Cousin Richard," entreated Mary, "find
another *vis-a-vis;* I ask to be excused this one
time."

"Certainly, if you wish it," replied the self-con-
stituted master of ceremonies, bowing coldly.

"What a handsome couple!" was the general
comment which ran in a whisper round the room
as they left.

"Harry is hovering on the brink, Dick," said
Copland; "if he fall in, good night."

"Caught in the toils," muttered Alloway to himself, "after the warning I gave him."

In the deserted drawing-room they found a secure
retreat from further interruption. Seating herself on
the sofa near one of the windows, Miss Littleton
artfully adjusted the folds of the thick damask curtain ostensibly, as her glance indicated, to screen
the couple from prying eyes, but really so as to
throw a shadowy veil over her face and thus enable
her to defy penetration into the workings of her
mind. Thus ensconced, with a queenly inclination she motioned her companion to a place
beside her, and asked with startling abruptness:

"Now, sir, what is it you would have of Mr.
Conrad?"

The question savored considerably of disdainful
hauteur.

"She treats me like an overgrown school boy,"
thought Carleton, instinctively rubbing his callow
chin; and, it must be confessed, appearances were

decidedly against our diplomatic neophyte's successful performance of his serious role.

" "I cannot hope to inspire you with the same degree of interest I feel in this affair," said he; "yet I may at least make bold to bespeak your sympathy in behalf of an infatuated fellow-creature who, following a whimsical humor of his own, is at last caught floundering in a bog of troubles."

"Say, rather, a star-gazing philosopher dropped into a well," replied the veiled beauty, in the same half scornful tone. . "Poor fellow! he has my heart-felt pity. Now for the cause of his sorrows?"

Thus conjured, Carleton rapidly and vividly portrayed the maze of difficulty in which he had become entangled, bringing forward in sharp relief the salient points which he considered. most likely to produce an effect upon his fair listener. Never was eloquent *raconteur* rewarded with more flattering attention. Impenetrably serene and still, she heard him through from beginning to end. He could not see her face distinctly, but the gentle heaving of her bosom betrayed no symptom of quickened pulsaton, and no unguarded gesture gave evidence of unusual excitement.

"Strange!" she said musingly, when he was done speaking, with a depth of feeling she had not before evinced. "He never said · a word to his nephew of his correspondence with Mr. Buchanan."

"So I conceived at first," said Carleton, adapting his language to her altered mood; "but, on after-thought, his silence does not appear to me in the least degree surprising. He was only solicitous to learn whether his former letter had reached its destination. Warned of his approaching end, it may be of the suddenness of the summons which awaited him, he sought to divert his mind wholly from worldly distractions, and to draw the curtain of oblivion on the painful past. His few remaining years were spent in preparing for the eternal scene; death was the familiar companion of his daily walks—the theme of his constant meditations. He lived as if the present moment might be the last of earth; and, although he was apparently free from mental disquietude, his soul was all the time paying cruel rack-rent for its battered tenement, and joyfully when the final notice came

'Left the warm precincts of the cheerful day,
Nor cast one longing, lingering look behind.'"

The melting pathos with which he rendered his brief tribute to the memory of her afflicted cousin went straight to her heart and dissipated every trace of cold reserve. Her manner was unaffectedly cordial and frank as she emerged from the curtained shadow and turned to him in the full-orbed radiance of her glorious beauty, "enough to make a world to doat."

"Many thanks, Mr. Carleton," she said, "for your entertaining story. It has interested me more than I have words to express. I sincerely wish you may be successful in your further researches. By all means I advise you to speak with Mr. Conrad. But, see the dance is over, and Lucy has promised to sing for us in the interlude."

So, after all, the diplomatist took nothing for his pains, though he was more than ever convinced that his fair listener was not a whit the wiser for his revelations.

"Who says a woman cannot keep a secret?" he mentally ejaculated. "Dissemblers by instinct, disguisers by habit, deceivers by intuition, they are masked batteries of deceitful wiles and delusive temptations; 'tis theirs to wheedle and cajole, to lurk in ambush for unwary man, and disarming his suspicions by flattery and blandishments, to shear him of his strength and deliver him over bound with wythes to his adversary. Delilahs all! Bah! what gammon! Man, the tyrant and despot of the sex, is alone responsible for the cajoleries, deceits and crafty recourses of woman. These are their only weapons of warfare, and whether their conduct be censurable or not, depends on the end to be gained."

With these incoherent and contradictory ideas chasing each other through his discomfited brain, he bowed his acknowledgments of her appreciative speech with graceful courtesy, and, resigning their seats to the tired dancers, they mingled with the joyous throng who were flocking around the sweet songstress already seated at the harpischord. She was turning over the leaves of a large new music book—Mr. Copland's present—as the truants approached.

"Come, Mary," she said, "choose a song for me."

But her father's cheery voice anticipated Mary's selection; the whist party had adjourned to hear her sing—"Rax me the beuk, bairn. There is a sang for you. I'se warrant, nane o' them ·has heard it."

The enchantress obeyed his command, and presently the touching strains of "Auld Robin Gray" fell upon the entranced ears of the company in a, shower of melodious tears. Everybody was in ecstacies. Even the flinty-hearted "Exciseman," between the music and the punch-bowl, grew rapturously lachrymose, and, forgetting his so-called official dignity, kissed the fair performer on both her blushing cheeks. Other songs were called for in quick succession, and were rendered in a way that, to our taste, was the perfection of music married to immortal verse.

At length the obliging Lucy had to give over from sheer exhaustion of fatigue, and, be it recorded for an example worthy of imitation on like occasions, no importunity could prevail with one of the other less gifted daughters of song there assembled to break the dulcet charm she had woven. We cannot stay to dwell on each delightful feature of this festive scene. A sterner task imperatively claims our attention. In diversions such as we feebly described, interlarded with a profusion of creature comforts, the tide of enjoyment flowed on in an unbroken stream to a late hour of the night. Instead of his national *Tullochgorum*, Mr. Graeme was well content to let young folks and old frisk through the intricacies of the Virginia reel, and when the merry guests took their leave, Lucy had abundant cause for unalloyed satisfaction. Mr. Waddell might come now and welcome.

"Dick," said Carleton, with a sleepy yawn, as they were riding slowly home, "Mary Littleton is, as you say, a beautiful enigma. I have lost the wager."

"I am glad of it," was the consoling reply, and the matter was dropped.

CHAPTER XV.

IT was well nigh day-break when the two friends arrived home from the party at Bonhill. Harry did not wait to be invited, but went straight to bed, and was soon lost to the music of the cock's shrill clarion and echoing horn. Not so Mr. Richard Alloway; he had other business on his hands. It was his rule not to permit the pursuit of pleasure at any time to interfere with the regular routine of his domestic administration. Social indulgences were never by him carried to an excess which unfitted him for the performance of his daily avocations with scrupulous exactitude. So, donning his workyday clothes, he called up the servant, who was sleeping by the fire in the hall, ordered a fresh horse, and sallied forth on his accustomed round. In addition to the ordinary tasks, there was a stalled ox to be slain that morning, an operation which he always superintended in proper person. The first faint streaks of the dawn were glimmering in the east, the air was crisp and frosty, and a soft, feathery mist hovered above the earth,

making the dark wood appear like an enchanted
island in the midst of a vapory sea.

> "Silent was then the forest bound,
> Save the red breast's note and the rustling sound
> Of frost-nipped leaves that are dropping around,
> Or the deep-mouthed cry of the distant hound
> That opens on his game."

What a morning for a fox-hunt, was Alloway's
first thought; his next was for a ride, and turning
into the road which led through the wood, he gave
the rein to his horse, and went dashing along at
a pace which soon stirred the sluggish blood into
a warm glow. As he came in sight of the main
highway, the dim outline of a human form whisked
rapidly across the open space in front of him. He
saw it only for a second; but there could be no
mistaking that burly frame and rolling gait.

"Ship ahoy!" shouted Dick, in a voice which
made the leaves rustle and quiver on the trees.

The figure halted suddenly, and was heard panting and blowing like a porpoise.

"Hilloa, ye bloody ould buccaneer, where the
divil are ye cruising to this time o' the morning?"
was Mr. Alloway's best essay at an Irish saluta-
tion, as he rode up to the old sailor.

"Och, Misther Dick," replied Mike, slowly regaining his presence of mind; "and its only yourself to be sure. Bad cess—I mane top o' the
mornin' and the blessin' o' St. Patrick to your
honor; but you've knocked me down on my bame
ends intirely."

"Hulled you at the first shot, and made you

round to in a hurry; rather ticklish for a crazy
old ship under a full press of sail, eh? Well, you
are my prize, Mike, and I shall see you safe into
port. You are the very man I was looking for.
So, vast heave; put your helm up or down, any
way you please, so you steer a bee-line for Woodbourne house."

While Dick was rattling on in this comical vein,
the umquihile Jack-tar was holding fast to both
his sides and · struggling hard to recover breath
sufficient to give utterance to the contending emotions which convulsed his sturdy form and imparted to his countenance a fearful expression,
somewhat rueful and exceeding wroth. On the
ground at his feet lay a rusty old Brown Bess of
a musket, which he eyed vengefully. Dick had not
observed him closely before, owing to the dimness
of the light.

"Och, the murtherin', thievin' vaggabins, Misther
Dick," he at length blurted out, and paused for a
fresh start.

"Who, Mike? Why, what on earth is the matter
with you?" asked Dick, eagerly; he had never seen
the old sailor in such a passion before.

"Matther wid me? Ye may well ask that; an'
sure wouldn't it be matther enough if the moradin'
villains had run away with your honor's own beautiful boat? By the bones uv my ancestors, it is
myself that will be afther purshuin' the dirty
blackguards to the ind o' the world, an' my name
is not Michael Burke."

"Not afoot and overland, Mike?" said Dick, repressing an inclination to laugh. "Come, tell me

16*

what has happened to put you in such a terrible stew."

Thus entreated, Mike, with many ejaculations of rage and a free use of the choicest epithets his vocabulary of nautical maledictions afforded, related his pitiful story. He could not tell precisely what was the hour, but it was after midnight last gone, that he was awaked by the furious barking of his faithful house-dog, which told as plainly as if the animal had spoken the words that there were thieves about. Jumping out of bed, he ran to the window in time to see a party of strange men making off with his boat, which was kept moored in a small cove at the foot of the garden. To snatch up his gun and rush to the door, all un-mindful of the plight he was in, was the work of an instant; but, before he could raise the latch, his wife awoke in a great fright, and, with a loud screech, at one bound precipitated herself upon him and immediately went into violent hysterics. She had taken due advantage of Mike's helpless condi-tion on retiring for the night to give him a piece of her mind, and now she was convinced her long-suffering spouse was meditating summary revenge; so she clung to him like grim death, weeping and praying, and howling and begging for mercy all in a breath. It was a fortunate diversion for the marauders; as by the time Mike had succeeded in assuring "swate Misthress Murchuson" that she was not the object of his murderous thoughts, and to make her understand what was the real cause of alarm, the boat had cleared the mouth of the cove and was safe from pursuit. But Mike had not been a bold sea-rover for nothing. He watched the "bloody pirates" until they were out of sight, and the water being as smooth as glass and the stars shining brightly, he had no trouble in seeing them, when they had gotten an offing, lay their course for the mouth of the Potomac river. His plan was conceived and put in execution with a celerity and vigor which would have reflected honor on the bold and enterprising commander of the *Endeavor* himself. Shouldering his trusty musket, and giving Mrs. Murchuson a wide berth for fear she might offer to interpose an obstacle to his design, he scudded away under full sail for the neighboring port of entry, where he was sure to find the assistance he needed in carrying his rapidly concocted plan into effect.

"You can count on me for help, heart and hand, old friend," exclaimed Alloway, when the sailor had finished his tale. "Hurry forward and have everything in readiness; I will join you without delay," and, speeding Mike on his way, he hastened homeward.

At the lawn gate he met James, the butler, who was looking for him with a note, which had just that moment been brought by a servant from Clifton. The bearer said his orders were to take it as quickly as possible to Mr. Alloway, and not to tarry for an answer. Dick glanced at the superscription; it was from Mary Littleton. With an explanation of surprise he hastily opened the letter, and read the following alarming summons:

"DEAR COUSIN RICHARD:

"Please come to me as speedily as you can. Something dreadful has happened; I know not what. Don't delay; every moment is as precious as life.

"Your distressed cousin,

"MARY LITTLETON."

"Good heavens!" thought Alloway, what can be to pay at Clifton?" But there was no time for speculation. His gallantry alone would have prompted immediate obedience to his cousin's command; but, from his knowledge of her firm and courageous temper, he was forced to conclude that this bewildering missive was far from being the inspiration of the ordinary pangs and fears which wars and women are said to have in common.

"James," said he to the servant, "go tell your Uncle William he need not wait for me, and see that Mr. Carleton is not disturbed until I get back. Stay—there is another thing I was near forgetting. Get a horse, and ride as fast as you can on the road to Yeocomico until you overtake Mr. Burke. Tell him not to stop for me; he'll understand. That's all I have to say," he added, seeing the man was hesitating for further orders, and plunging into a nigh path through the wood he proceeded to obey Miss Littleton's mandate at the top of his horse's speed.

The excitement of a night's frolicking is not conducive of sound slumber. Such was Carleton's experience when he found himself wide awake after

having slept an hour or two, little refreshed and
the prey of nervous restlessness. His senses were
not yet recovered from the giddy whirl of intoxi-
cation, and the gay and merry scenes he had just
quitted danced before his eyes in a wild phantas-
magoria of revelry. One object only was clearly
discernible in the ever-shifting maze of fancy, a
picture never to be erased from memory—which
"seen became a part of sight"—that of the daz-
zling vision of womanly perfection, the queenly
creature who had sat and listened so intently to
his strange story, her glorious eyes shining like
stars in the dusky twilight sky, and her head
resting on one fair hand which pressed back the
luxuriant mass of hair she suffered with careless
art to float in rich undulations over her neck and
shoulders. Beyond the lingering sense of sore
chagrin at the failure of his deep-laid scheme to
surprise her heart's secret, he did not try to
analyze the sensations, very near akin to love, with
which she had inspired him. He was convinced by
that one interview that the interesting stranger was
master of the situation, and he was not the man
"to build a fair house on another man's ground."

Finding it utterly vain trying to woo the drowsy
god back again, he arose, dressed in haste, and descended to the hall. Seeing nobody stirring about
the house, he concluded his host was still a-bed,
and that the best thing he could do to while
away the time until Alloway made his appearance,
was to take another leisurely survey of that charming pleasure ground—the library. This time it is
the books which attract his particular regard. Of

these there are a great variety—principally standard works in every department of letters, and many of them exceedingly rare and curious specimens. Mr. John Austin was something of a bibliophile, and, although he did not exactly regard everything as fish which came to his net, he was far from indulging the "hide-bound humor" of a severely censorious judgment in gathering his supplies of mental pabulum. Evidently he thought, with his favorite author, that he could not more safely and with less danger scout into the regions of sin and falsity than by reading all manner of disquisitions, and hearing all manner of reason. The valuable collection was mainly the result of his liberal disposition and untiring industry, but his son had enriched it by the addition of the most recent English and French publications.

What were Carleton's sensations as he gazed wistfully at this rich mine of treasured lore? While at College he had frequently been heard to declare that it was the darling object of his ambition to become a distinguished scholar—to erect an enduring monument of his fame in that congenial field of intellectual enterprise. But another career was marked out for him by the hand of overruling destiny. From blissful academic dreams, he has been rudely awakened by the rush and roar of angry, surging waters. In the vortex of a mighty revolution he must plunge, and, Percy-like, drag up drown'd honor by the locks. Young as he was, he was well fitted to bear an active and shining part in the stirring events of the period. The faculties of some men are developed with amazing precocity.

At an early age, before they have reached the arbitrary limit of parental pupilage, their matchless
powers seem to have attained the fullest stature,
and they need only the spur of opportunity to call
them into vigorous play. Experience is, indeed, in-
dispensable to the complete fruition of genius; it
corrects the judgment, informs the understanding,
enlarges the heart, and chastens the spirit, incul-
cating prudence and enforcing the necessity of vigilant self-control. But while it points out the true
mark and gives steadiness to the aim, it adds
nothing to the strength of the arm that bends the
springing bow. That is the jealous boon of the
Almighty Giver bestowed for great purposes on the
chosen instruments of providential design. To this
favored class, the eagles of their kind, belonged
Henry Carleton. To a joyous and sanguine temperament, and a ready and sparkling wit, he united
a judgment sagacious, ripe and discerning beyond
his years, a daring and determined spirit, and a
soul which glowed with the vestal fire of sincerely
patriotic devotion. With such qualities, it is no
wonder that in after years he won the intimate
confidence and friendship of the most severely just
judge of the motives and conduct of his fellows—
"the man who was first in war, first in peace,
and first in the hearts of his countrymen." It is
true, he does not appear to be directly involved
with the train of circumstances which form the
ground work of the present narrative; yet we have
thought proper to accord him a passing tribute,
and to express the hope that his appearance in
ever so subordinate a part on our mimic stage may

afford some foreshadowing of the character he displayed in real action.

On this occasion our cavalier seems to be greatly puzzled to find such light diversion as accords with the excited frame of his mind. At length he selects at random a volume of the handsome new edition of Pope, which is a portion of Mr. Richard Austin's latest contributions to the stock of miscellaneous literature. It is all correspondence. There is a folded page on which a passage has been marked with a pencil. He reads it aloud: "Great God! what an incongruous animal man is! How unsettled in his best part, his soul, and how changeable and variable in his frame of body; the constancy of the one shook by every notion, the temperament of the other affected by every blast of wind. What is he altogether but one inconsistency? Sickness and pain are the lot of one-half of him; doubt and fear the portion of the other. What a bustle we make about passing our time, when all our span is but a point. What aims and ambitions are crowded in this little instant of our life which is rounded with a sleep. Our whole extent of being is no more in the eye of Him who gave it than a scarce perceptible moment of duration. Those animals whose circle of being is limited by three or four hours, as the naturalists tell us, are yet as long-lived and possess as wide a scene of action as man, if we consider him with a view to all space and all eternity. Who knows what plots, what achievements a mite may perform in his kingdom of a grain of dust within his life of some minutes, and of how much less consideration than tĥis is the life of man in the sight of God, who is from ever and forever! Who that thinks in this train but must see the world and its contemptible grandeurs lessen before him at every thought. 'Tis enough to make our brains stupefied in a poize of inaction, void of all desires, of all delights, of all friendships."

Carleton mused: "'Twere a twinge indeed, thought he, could extort such a lugubrious note as this from the sweet swan of Twickenham. He must have been woefully haunted with blue-devils. Could it be imagined that the maudlin creature who vented this nauseating rheum of splenetic humor was the same author who wrote the "Messiah" and the "Essay on Man?" A pitiable world it would be if everybody in it moralized in so desponding and distempered a train. It is a blessed thing that man is an incongruous animal—many sided, many handed, and many minded; if he were not, what a humdrum affair would be the epic of human life? For all the snarling of mangy cynics, he is a most marvellous piece of mechanism, well deserving the eulogy of the divinest of bards—"noble in reason, infinite in faculties, in form and moving, how express and admirable, in action how like an angel, in apprehension how like a god!" Such is the light in which he should be taught to regard himself, and without the just pride which is the manifestation of the Divinity which stirs within him, he would be more despicable than the tiniest midge that disports its brief hour in the sunbeam."

"It is to be hoped," he continued, speaking aloud, "that Mr. Richard Austin was not prevailed

17

upon to swallow such empirical stuff as an anti-
dote for the bane of a miserable life. Dick's a
happy fellow; how I envy him his knack of taking
the world so easy. Had this peripatetic personage
been my uncle, I would not have had a day's
peace of mind until I had fully realized the folly
of that wisdom which is to be had by prying into
forbidden secrets. Call it what you will, childish
superstition, idle curiosity—but if this old house
belonged to me, it should be made to give up its
secret, or else I would blow it up with gun-
powder."

"Playing Guy Fawkes, eh?" cried a voice behind
him.

CHAPTER XVI.

T was Alloway who had come hurriedly into the room unperceived. Carleton started at the sudden apparition. "Why, Dick," he exclaimed, "I thought you were all this time fast asleep, and here you are looking as if you had been riding a steeple-chase, and you are as solemn as an owl and as mysterious as the devil. Hang it all! Don't stand there gaping like a moon-calf in a dumb show, but out with it at once. What in the world have you been doing?"

"In a moment, Harry." He went out, gave an order to the servant and returned. "Now," said he, "sit down and let me have your undivided attention. It is a real mystery this time; I sincerely trust it may not lead to a tragical disclosure."

"He is evidently in earnest," thought Carleton, seating himself in the nearest chair, *arrectis auribus.*

"Read that," said Dick, giving him Miss Littleton's note, by way of dramatic prologue.

On perusing it the last shade of incredulity vanished from his brow; he listened eagerly. Briefly

recounting the occurrences we have narrated, Alloway went on to say: "When I arrived at Clifton
I found my cousin waiting for me in the parlor.
She was very pale, but perfectly composed and
self-possessed. It is surprising what wonderful command over their feelings some women have. After
thanking me in one earnest word for my prompt-
ness, she at once made known the reason of her
importunate message. Colonel Littleton and herself
were the last of the company to leave Bonhill, she
having lingered to speak with Mrs. Graeme. On
reaching home, she had barely gone to her room
before she heard the furious galloping of a horse,
and, as it stopped in front of the door, a voice,
which she instantly recognized as Mr. Thompson's,
bawled out: 'Littleton, Littleton!' Her father had
not quitted the hall, and going quickly to the
door exclaimed, as he opened it and caught sight
of the collector, 'My God, neighbor, what is the
matter with you?' Alarmed, she ran to the window and looked out. There sat old Jake on his
horse, a figure to look upon. He was in a state of
excitement bordering on phrensy; his features were
convulsed with rage, and he was talking and ges-
ticulating at a fearful rate. She could not make
out what he was saying, farther than that something was the matter with Archie, and now and
then she was convinced that she caught an un-
complimentary allusion to her father's guest. Presently, he wheeled his horse around, and, throwing a
parting word over his shoulder, went flying down
the avenue with break-neck speed. Hurrying down
stairs, she met her father. She had never seen him
more agitated and distressed. 'This is a terribly

bad business, my daughter,' he said. 'Thompson's little boy has been spirited away—carried off in the night; two of his hands are reported to be missing, and he himself is as mad as a March hare, for he swears that Mr. Conrad is the cause of it all.' Well nigh fainting with apprehension and alarm—any other woman would have swooned away on the spot—she besought him to tell her how it happened. He replied that he could not get a clear or definite account from the Collector, he raved so incoherently; but, at her earnest entreaty, he very promptly ordered his horse and set out in pursuit of his demented neighbor. When he was gone, her fears increased, and, in her extremity, she sent for me. You remember that fellow we saw yesterday on the river in a skiff?"

Carleton.—"The sailor? Yes, and the boy also."

Alloway.—"The villain was following Archie, and if any harm has befallen the poor lad he is probably the author of it." Here he related the adventure of the oak, with which the reader is familiar.

Carleton.—"No doubt the rascal had a hand in it—very likely the principal; but he must have had help in such a daring undertaking."

Dick.—"Precisely what the Collector said, only he accuses Mr. Conrad of being the primo mover in the scheme of villainy, and that was the greatest source of trouble to my fair cousin, as much as she felt on Archie's account. 'Nothing,' said she, 'could be more absolutely false, not to say preposterous.' I do not know what possessed me, but I started to say something about the suspected party being a stranger, and immediately wished the words

17*

had choked me. 'Stay,' she cried—and you should
have seen how the blood rushed into her face and
then flowed back upon her heart, leaving her as
white as an alabaster figure, while her eyes sparkled
and flashed like two great diamonds—'I know what
it is you would say. Stranger let him be; but, for
the sake of your own dear honor, breathe not a
syllable of the unjust suspicion which your looks
imply. It is no time for explanations. Still as I
have invited this conference in a matter of the
most delicate and distressing nature, you have a
right to expect my entire confidence shall be given
you. In due time you will be fully gratified. For
the present it is enough for you to know that he
in whose behalf I bespeak your interest is my
affianced husband, the peer of the best gentleman
in the land.' Jupiter, how splendidly she said that,
and how thoroughbred she looked!"

Seeing Carleton smile at this last characteristic
simile, he quickly continued, "It was impossible to
gainsay this candid declaration. The starch was
completely taken out of me. I felt an indescribable
thrill of sympathy and admiration, and hastened to
assure my lovely cousin that my poor service was
entirely at her command. And had she ordered me
to bring her the head of the Grand Turk, I should
have started, I verily believe, post-haste for Con-
stantinople on horseback."

"*O Dea certe!* What a wonderful metamorphosis
the heartless coquette has undergone!" Carleton
could not resist the temptation of saying.

"I deserve your ill-timed sarcasm, Harry," said
the penitent Richard, "but I beg you will not again
interrupt me. As I was saying, I asked her how I

could best aid her in the matter. She replied that Mr. Conrad was now at Yeocomico, whither he went yesterday afternoon on business. He was expected back some time during the morning. Of this her father knew nothing. She wished that I would seek him as speedily as possible, and apprise him of what has happened before that hot-headed old blunderbuss of a tory brings the hue and cry of the country about his ears—a result which would exasperate the high-spirited gentleman .beyond endurance, besides being to her mortifying in the extreme. This I readily undertook to do, and seeing that she had glanced repeatedly at the clock and noted every swing of the pendulum, 'one word more,' said I; 'may I take Mr. Carleton with me?' 'As you please,' said she; and off I went like a shot, and here I am, and breakfast is ready, and our horses are at the door. You see, Harry," added Dick, persuasively, "it is a ticklish piece of business, and I shall need your tact to help me through with it."

"Anything to oblige you, Dick," said Carleton; "but I must confess that the salt has lost its savor. Miss Littleton's affianced husband! I'm sped; ''tis not so deep as a well, nor so wide'— say, Dick, why not let the old tory and the Frenchman fight it out *a-la-mort?*"

"Come, Harry," replied his host with dignity; "it is no time for pleasantry. I feel acutely for Mr. Thompson, and do earnestly hope that nothing evil has happened to poor little Archie."

"I stand reproved, Dickon," protested Carleton, "so, *en avant!*"

CHAPTER XVII.

THE morning meal hurriedly partaken, Alloway and Carleton mounted their fleet steeds, and in nowhile gained the summit of the high hill within a mile of the port of entry, from which was a full view of the broad Potomac. The first object which greeted their sight on its placid bosom was the gallant bark *Katrine*, looming upon the horizon like some "huge bird of heavenly plumage fair," every stitch of her canvas being flung out to catch the light breeze. At this stage, the intersection of two roads, they were joined by another horseman, who came thundering along the highway known as the "Neck" road, bloody with spurring, fiery-red with speed.

"Jupiter!" exclaimed Alloway, "if it is not the Collector."

It was indeed Mr. Jacob Thompson, still in a towering rage and looking the incarnation of vengeance and destruction. His clothes, which had not been changed since the party, were scarcely distinguishable in pattern for the mud with which he was covered from head to foot; his gaunt and burly form trembled with passion, and he shook his clenched hand at the ship, shouting as he did so with the cry of a baffled tiger:

"Gone, by God! the infernal black pirate."

"For Heaven's sake, Mr. Thompson," cried the friends in a breath, "what is the meaning of this pother?"

"O, you marauding scoundrel!" exclaimed the irate old gentleman, taking no notice of the question; "I'll be even with you yet. I'll live to see you hanging like a dog at the yard-arm of your own vessel."

"Who is it?" inquired Dick, eagerly; "surely not Captain Dent?"

"It is Dent, sir," roared the Collector, as if he defied Dick to deny it; "Dent, the deceitful, palavering, kidnapping villain."

Dick.—"Kidnapping! Have they carried Archie off in the vessel?"

Collector.—"Archie is gone, sir; and, what is more, two of my best hands."

"Dunmore's proclamation," chimed in the mischievous Carleton, by way of adding fuel to the flame of the old gentleman's wrath.

"D—n Dunmore!" he exclaimed; "the blackhearted, white-livered poltroon. He ran away at the first gun, and left the like of me to the tender mercies of rebels, thieves and murderers. He will get his deserts when the King hears of these outrages. Haven't you brought the country to a pretty pass among you? No law, no officers, no anything—just a d—d den of savages and wild beasts.

You go and kick up a row because you want to live without paying your taxes to the government you belong to; and this man they call a governor gets scared and sneaks off, and then calls upon the negroes to help him. A pretty way to put down one rebellion by raising a worse; and he never once asks leave of their owners whether they be loyal men or not. He shall be impeached as sure as there is a Parliament sitting in London."

Seeing that the old gentleman was so beside himself with anger that nothing was to be gotten from him but an incoherent tirade of abuse of everybody and everything, Alloway thought to divert the tide of his wrath by saying that Carleton and he were out in search of Mr. Conrad. It was the signal of another explosion.

"Looking for him, are you? Then you may as well turn round and go back home. You'll not see the rascal again in a hurry, I'll be bound. I knew him for a d—d French spy as soon as I set eyes on him; I said as much to Littleton. Eh! Why, there he is now."

It was not Conrad as the friends naturally surmised, but Colonel Littleton, approaching them from the direction of Yeocomico. As he rode up his greeting was constrained and embarrassed, and although he tried hard to master his emotion, perplexity and chagrin were plainly visible in his face.

"You are early abroad after the frolic last night, young gentlemen," said he to Alloway and Carleton, and then, as the former was about to reply, turning quickly to Mr. Thompson, he continued, "Come, neighbor, it's no use tarrying here; I'll see you home."

The Collector gave a vengeful glance at the *Katrine*. She had by this time rounded Smith's Point, and was standing down the bay. Then, without a word, he accepted Colonel Littleton's proposal, and they rode away together. Recovering from his surprise, Alloway called to Colonel Littleton to inquire whether he had seen or heard aught of Mr. Conrad in his ride.

"He's gone!" replied the 'Squire, sharply and without turning his head.

The young cavaliers sat regarding each other in blank astonishment.

"Well, Harry," said Dick, drawing in a deep breath, and emitting it in a most musical, most melancholy whistle, "what's to be done now?"

Even the quick-witted Carleton was for once dumbfounded. "Would it were bed-time and all were well," he was in the act of saying, when he was interrupted by a hoarse voice calling: "O, Mr. Richard, I certainly am glad to see you," and at the same moment an old man, dressed like a fisherman, shambled out of a thicket near the road and stood before them. He stuck the paddle, which he carried on his shoulder, in the ground, and leant on it with both hands.

"Good morning, Mr. Bragg," said Dick; "you seem tired."

"An' well I mought be," replied the fisherman; "I have walked every blessed step of the way from my house, as hard as I could put foot to the ground, with this here letter for Mr. Graum, which it was sent to him by a gentleman on board of the vessel, and he told me to be sure he got it betimes this morning. Now, Mr. Richard, if you be going soon—,"

"I can save you the rest of the journey? Certainly," replied Alloway, taking the letter from the old man's hand; "so you saw the *Katrine* off?"

Bragg.—"Yes, sir; I was 'long side of her when she weighed anchor. You see, the Captain wanted me to bring him some oysters."

Dick.—"Had she many passengers?"

Bragg.—"I can't speak for certain about that. I didn't see nobody but the Scotch gentleman as give me the letter. There was two niggers in a big boat beggin' and entreatin' of the Captain in the pitifullest manner to take 'em on board; but he told 'em to go back home and give his respecks to their master and tell him he wasn't in the nigger kidnappin' business at this pertickler time. While they was a chaffin, I seen another big boat come out of the creek. Soon as ever them darkies got sight of her they 'peared to know eggzactly what was to pay, for they let go the painter and shot for shore 'way up the river. Then come the chase,—"

"Thank you, Mr. Bragg, that's all I wish to know," said Dick, preparing to go.

"Hold on one second, Mr. Richard," said the fisherman; "what *is* the matter with Mr. Thompson? He come straining by me like he wan't caring if he killed his horse or broke his own neck."

"They were his negroes who were running away," replied Alloway, and commending the loquacious fisherman to a more appreciative audience, he and

Carleton were off again on the wings of the wind.
They separated at the road leading to Woodbourne,
Alloway proceeding directly to Bonhill.

The day was now far spent; Mr. Graeme was
not long returned from his usual ride. Discarding
ceremony, the young man rushed into his presence
and, thrusting the letter into his hand, exclaimed:
"For Heaven's sake, Mr. Graeme, tell me quickly
what news is in it."

The good gentleman stared at his excited neighbor as if he thought he had surely *"gane gyte;"* but
he was so completely knocked off his balance as to
be incapable of resenting the indecorous proceeding.
Hastily breaking the seal, he ran his eye over the
letter in search of the explanation of this un-
gracious intrusion on his privacy. Suddenly his
manner changed; he became fearfully agitated, and
his countenance betrayed a variety of indescribable
emotions. Recovering his habitual self-control by a
strong effort, he slowly and attentively reperused
the letter, and, having done so, remained some
minutes in deep thought. Then he rose from his
chair, and, turning to Alloway, said in a calm and
decided tone: "Bide here a time, Richard, lad;
aiblins ye might wish to speak a word wi' Lucy;
but ye maunna be ganging hame before my return
frae Clifton;" and before his visitor could utter a
word in reply, he snatched up his hat and cane
and left the room. In the hall he met his daughter,
to whom he communicated something in a low,
earnest tone, and ere another hour elapses, he is
seen in close conference with Mary Littleton and
her father.

18

CHAPTER XVIII.

THOROUGHLY worn down by the day's rough work, Carleton as soon as he reached Woodbourne threw himself to rest on the settle in the library. "Well," said he, "this beats cock-fighting out of sight, as Bob Temple would say, and fox-hunting, too, from the way my limbs ache; just enough of the flavor of villainy to give it relish. What can that rascally skipper be up to? Mary Littleton's fiancée has decamped, too; the old, sorrowful story; it's a sad business; yet, what's the loss of one lover to a girl who has a pack of them that will come at her whistle? Who knows that it may not yet be my turn? Psha! I verily believe I am getting to be as big a ninny as the rest of them. *Amour tu perdis Troie!* A deep saying that of the divine Pascal; there's indeed no guessing what would have happened to the human family had Madam Cleopatra's nose been a little shorter. Heigh ho! This is excellent sport for the piping times of peace; but it is not the way to purge these English hence. Shame upon the whole tribe of lusty young fel-

lows, myself among the number, to be dancing
attendance here on a pair of black or blue eyes, or
else galloping over the country after hounds and
horn, when they should be in the trenches at
Boston with muskets in their hands. But Rome
was not built in a day; neither can a cavalry
company be recruited and equipped for service in
the twinkling of an eye. I have gained one important point. Alloway has engaged to help me,
and he is a tower of strength. I have always entertained a warm regard for Dick's amiable qualities, but I had no conception before of the amount
of good, stern stuff that was in him. Bold, alert,
sharp-sighted and strong-limbed, he is a born stark
trooper. I wish I had a hundred just like him
enlisted for the war and determined to fight to the
bitter end." With which patriotic aspiration his
soliloquy ended, and another minute he was fast
locked in the embrace of the drowsy god.

He had been scarcely an hour asleep before he
was awakened by the entrance of a visitor. It was
the young lawyer. He, too, showed evident signs
of having been considerably jostled from his usual
placid and sedate demeanor.

"All alone, Harry?" he exclaimed, barely giving
Carleton time to say good morning. "Where's Alloway? What's all the muss about? The whole
country is up in arms, but devil a soul can tell
what it means. Dick, they say, is in the secret;
where can I find him?"

Here James, who had ushered in Mr. Copland,
explained the cause of his master's detention at
Bonhill.

"But he must have told you everything, Harry; that's the next best evidence. Tell me, now, the exact truth of the matter; I have had enough of Temple's palaver."

"What I know is soon told," replied Carleton. "It seems that this Captain Dent, with what motive is beyond conjecture, has abducted old Mr. Thompson's foster-son, and it is moreover surmised by some people that a certain foreign adventurer, in whom a lady acquaintance of ours is said to be interested, had a hand in the nefarious transaction."

Copland.—"The Frenchman? Why, Bob Temple just now informed me that he and Miss Littleton were engaged to be married."

Harry.—"The tattling coxcomb! What does he know about it?"

Copland.—"Next to nothing, I am well satisfied, and therefore I shall have to call a more reliable and better informed witness. Come to the book, Harry. I must have the truth, the whole truth and nothing but the truth concerning that little tête-à-tête last night."

Evidently Carleton was not in a humor to relish his friend's bantering tone. He had suddenly lapsed into gravity. "No offence, Charley," he said, "but I must insist on dropping the subject; it sounds so unfeeling—our jesting—considering the turn things have taken. What you have heard is very true; they are betrothed. Dick Alloway had the assurance from Miss Littleton's own lips this morning. Why he went away on the vessel I cannot divine; but of one thing I have no manner of doubt—he is not implicated in the kidnapping affair."

Copland.—"It is a pretty case, Harry, and my professional acumen is greatly piqued; but since you wish it, I will forego the examination for the present. Gone, eh? taken French leave! What was the tune we were dancing to last night? 'Malbrook has gone to the wars.' A thousand pardons, Harry; what was you going to say?"

Harry.—"Having dismissed that disagreeable topic, tell me what is the news abroad. I did not have a chance to question you at the party last night."

Copland.—"My intelligence is summed up in one word—war; they mean to lick us into terms if they can. Such is the pronounced purpose of the Ministry, and the body of the people applaud it. During my three years' stay in London I was a close observer, and read with care the real expositors of public sentiment. The secret of Lord Chatham's popularity and influence lay in the unexampled success of his war policy, conducted as it was with such wonderful spirit and energy. The results added immensely to the British possessions, and placed the nation on the pinnacle of power and greatness. The land resounded with the *Io Triomphe* of the Great Commoner, the people's idol, a very god,—and what was of more importance to us, the sincere friend of America, inflexibly opposed to every scheme tending to subject us to unrighteous burthens. The jubilee over, the day for auditing arrives—the remorseless piper presents his bill. Lo, the budget foots up the enormous sum of £140,000,000—the whole of it spent by Lord Chatham in his glorious campaigns. He is naturally looked to for suggesting the way to pay it; but

18*

he is no financier; such drudgery is beneath the notice of a great statesman; he turns the business over to his brother-in-law, Granville. That minister tries the old-fashioned plan. New duties, imposts and excises are the order of the day. The country is in a ferment of indignation; the cities grow riotous, and Ciderland, especially, is ready to raise the standard of open rebellion. In despair, ministers resort to the colonies for help. These, they say, have been the sole gainers by the war, have been saved from the tender mercies of tomahawk and scalping-knife by British valor; they must foot the bill. The colonies flare up, and their attitude creates alarm among the merchant princes of London, Liverpool and Bristol. Granville points to the war-budget of his predecessor, and demands to know where he is to get money to meet the deficit in the treasury. Pitt retorts with a humorous sally, but the 'Gentle Shepherd' is not so easily laughed out of court. He reiterates the significant question, and sober business men realize its grave importance. It is plain to them that every source of legitimate revenue must be tapped or the credit of the nation will be irretrievably damaged. Thus the question of the right to tax the colonies became the one absorbing theme of parliamentary debate and popular agitation. In proportion to our earnestness in protesting against the outrage, did public opinion in England manifest itself in favor of the King's determination to make the experiment, and now the nation as a whole is, in my judgment, fully prepared to support the most vigorous measures the administration may devise for our subjugation. You can't imagine how contemptuously they speak of us. I was mad enough to fight a hundred times before I left London, but managed to keep my temper from getting the better of my discretion."

Harry.—"What you say corroborates Mr. Arthur Lee's opinion in a recent letter to my father. Well, I, for one, do not regret the course events have taken. With my good old preceptor, Dr. Witherspoon, I believe the people of America are not only ripe for independence but rotting. It is too late now for the government to retrace its steps. Our terms have risen since the guns opened on Boston. We can be satisfied with nothing less than the unequivocal renunciation of the right to tax us against our consent, and guaranteeing to us by irrepealable grants local home government, involving the retrenchment of the executive functions of vice-regents, and an increase of legislative authority in the provincial assemblies. In a word, we must have all and singular the privileges, immunities and franchises of English subjects. These they are not likely to give, and the end is foreseen. To your tents, O Israel!"

Copland.—"Why, Harry, you are an improved edition of Nat Bacon."

Harry (enthusiastically).—"You could not pay me a dearer compliment. Bacon fired the first gun for American liberty; may it be my glorious privilege to shoot the last mother's son of its enemies."

Copland (professional caution could not stand before the fiery zeal of his companion).—"You are a trump, Harry," he warmly replied. "Still I cannot help wishing the crisis had been put off until I

had finished the round of the inns of courts.
However, that's no great matter; this revolution, if
it succeeds, will make many sweeping changes in
the principles and practices of the common law,
and I may have to unlearn half I know at present.
But who have we here?"

It was another visitor come to learn the exact
particulars of that astounding outrage. Soon another
and another arrived in breathlesss haste. The
exciting news had flown far and wide over the
country; the untiring "postman" was in his element, doing yeoman service and sending the intelligence with lightning speed in every direction.
Gathering volume as it passed from mouth to
mouth, it at last swelled into the most extravagant
dimensions, past all whooping, and rumor after
rumor of the most absurd description glided swim-
mingly along on the top wave of popular credulity
to the remotest corner of the colony.

In no while Carleton found himself to be the
cynosure of quite an imposing assembly of indignant young patriots, who were unanimously agreed
that it was high time to put a stop to such high-
handed and lawless proceedings. He improved the
occasion to harangue them on the abominations of
tyranny in general, and the grievous oppressions of
British rule in particular. The fruits of his glowing phillippic were a round dozen able-bodied vol-
unteer recruits for the horse company.

It was after candle-light when Alloway returned;
the company were all gone, and Carleton was again
alone. His host was whistling as he entered, a
signal which foreboded other strange developments.

"Here you are at last!" cried Carleton, "charged to the muzzle with inscrutable wisdom, to judge from your looks. Come, out with it; I am heartily disgusted with this everlasting game of blind-man's buff."

"Blind-man's buff with a vengeance!" replied Dick, dropping into a chair and stretching his limbs with an air of intense weariness. "Throw me the slippers there in the corner. What a relief to get rid of these plaguey hard boots; now I am comfortable. Well, Harry, we are at a dead fault; the trail is as cold as a wedge—lost beyond recovery;" and, to give emphasis to the startling announcement, he stared hard at his friend with a visage that was comically blank and rueful.

Bewildered as he was, Carleton could not help laughing. "Lost!" he repeated; "where? in Mr. Graeme's punch-bowl?"

"In Chesapeake bay," replied Dick, with unmoved countenance; "the pirate has captured your mighty hero, and away goes your little romance. If I was not so sleepy, I would a tale unfold—"

Harry.—"Not a wink of sleep shall you have until you tell me what you know;" and suiting the action to the word, he locked the door of the room and put the key in his pocket.

Dick.—"And shall I not take mine ease in mine inn, Hal?"

Harry.—"When you have done with your provoking tomfoolery, not before. Come, sir, the story, the story!"

Dick.—"Sheath your impatience, Hal. Will not a song do as well? Captain Kidd, you know—

    "'And he sailed and he sailed—'"

Harry.—"I verily believe you are tipsy in good earnest. Your conduct is outrageous. Here I have been the best part of the day—(Dick, *sotto voce,* 'As dry as a powder-horn,')—entertaining a score or more of your friends and neighbors while you have been—"

Dick.—"In better company. Well, insatiable news-monger, sit down and hearken to my tale, and much may it enlighten you."

But highly as we respect Mr. Richard Alloway's powers of narration, we prefer to tell the story in our own way, and in our own good time.

CHAPTER XIX.

IN the Christian calendar, the Sabbath is the first day of the week. Of old, it was the seventh and last day which the Almighty Maker hallowed and blessed for His own. By the change it became doubly sanctified, celebrating the victory over death and the grave, and forever typical of the rest which is prepared for the saints in heaven.

It cannot be denied that very loose notions at this time prevailed in Virginia as to the due observance of the Lord's day, but with the exception of that phase of profanity more or less common to every age and country since the Christian era began, the people were duly regardful of everything that pertained to the sanctity of religious institutions.

It was Sunday, the last day of Carleton's proposed sojourn at Woodbourne, and, judging from the signs of the weather, it was the last, too, of that delightful interlude of the seasons which, in this latitude, goes by the name of the Indian Summer. The wind was blowing great guns from the northwest; cloudy

racks went skurrying across the welkin's face,
darkening the sun and shooting cold lances through
shivering lights and livers, and the leaves of the
forest were falling thick and fast under the savage
flail of the tempest. Harry was sitting at the window watching the limbs of the great oak on the
lawn, as they swayed to and fro in the gale.

"I am thinking there will be a slim attendance
at church this blustering morning," said he, turning to Dick, who had just come in and was
toasting his shins by the fire.

"Never you fear for that," replied his friend.
"Between curiosity to hear the 'new-light' preacher,
and the desire to talk over yesterday's doings, they
won't mind the weather if the wind does blow.
Ugh! but it's a nipper nevertheless, right from the
North Pole."

Harry.—"It will be as great a treat to me as
to the rest of the benighted heathen hereabouts. I
haven't heard a good rousing sermon since I left
Nassau Hall. Mr. Waddell is said to be a man of
extraordinary parts; he'll be sure to stir things up
from the bottom. You will catch it, you miserable
sinner."

Dick.—"For what, more than the rest of you?"

Harry.—"Why, for your two notoriously beset-
ting sins—horse-racing and fox-hunting."

Dick.—"If that's all, let it blow till it crack. I
do certainly love a fine horse, and can boast of
the fastest to be found in the four counties. As
for fox-hunting, I freely confess that I am somewhat addicted to the good old gentlemanly pastime
which has come down to us from remotest an-

tiquity, and which, by the bye, was especially honored by your mighty hero, Harry the Fifth of England."

Harry.—"I never heard before that he was so passionately fond of the chase. Where did you get your information?"

Dick.—"Not from Shakespeare! Still it is a historical fact. Why, did you never read the story of his coming one day to see his darling Kate in Paris with a fox-tail stuck in his helmet in place of a plume? What did that signify, I should like to know?"

Harry.—"Rightly interpreted, it meant that he had won the brush—that is to say, the wife and her rich dowry of lands, chattels and hereditaments."

Dick.—"Anyhow, it was a royal recognition of the glorious sport which has always been the pride and delight of free-born Britons. The preachers had as well be done canting about the cruelty of it. What were birds and beasts of prey—dogs and men included—made for but to exterminate pestiferous vermin and keep the world from being overrun by vegetarians and herbivorists? It is ridiculous, past endurance to hear one of these sleek parsons, whose paunch is with 'good, fat capon lined,' and whose life is one happy dream of green goose and chicken-pie, railing at the barbarous custom of destroying the poor innocent foxes."

Harry (laughing).—"You are perfectly incorrigible, Dick. You wouldn't dare to make that speech in Mr. Graeme's hearing."

19

Dick—"Why not? The old gentleman is as keen a sportsman as any of us. You would be charmed to hear him describe his famous badger-hunts when he was a pranksome lad in Scotland. But it's time we were getting ready for church."

In the midst of what was once a magnificent grove of oaks and hickories, cedars and poplars, hard by a spring of the purest and coolest water that ever refreshed the thirst of man and beast, rises a venerable pile dedicated long years ago by Christian prayers to the worship of the living God. The date is on the wall. It was built A. D. 1706, of bricks, they say, brought all the way from England, hard enough when they came out of their native kiln, but so much the harder for their sea-change as to defy the ravages of old Edax Tempus. It is in much better preservation than many similar edifices in Virginia of much later date of erection, and has undergone occasional repairs and alterations from time to time. Some of these betterments had better been left off, in our opinion. A new roof was indispensably necessary; but, alas, the sacreligious genius of modern improvement has gone inside and ransacked and disfigured at such a tasteful rate that the original architect would not be able to recognize his goodly handiwork. Especially do we miss from its place the quaint old-fashioned pulpit, with its overhanging sounding-board, which, in the wantonness of juvenile fancy, we expected to see come down like a well-fitting lid and imprison the Rev. Thumbtext in a living tomb. Mayhap the dread of such a catastrophe led to its removal. Outside everything speaks of ruin

and decay. The wall, which enclosed a space of
two acres, in the centre of which stands the
church, has crumbled to the earth in a dozen
places; the vestry-room is a dismantled wreck,
fragments of broken tombstones are strewn around,
and the frequent yawning hollows within the pale
remind the passenger how soon he may be the
prey of dumb forgetfulness. The old church has
seen strange sights in its day, and experienced a
variety of uses little dreamed of by its pious
founders. In the war of 1812, as many living witnesses can testify, it furnished commodious quarters
for a squad of valorous militiamen, charged with
the duty of watching the enemy's war vessels,
which were constantly running in and out of the
river and sending their barges ashore to set fire to
houses and hay-stacks. They performed their part
like veterans, if we are to believe the stories of
their prowess related by a surviving member; on
one occasion actually marching ten miles in a
single night, and reaching their destination in time
to cook their breakfast by the smoldering embers
of a once proud mansion, and to fire a volley—of
oaths—at the hindmost sloop-of-war now hull-down
on the horizon. Then it became by day a school-
house, where young ideas were trained to such ex-
pertness in throwing stones as not to leave a whole
pane of glass in the large mullioned windows;
and at night it served as a grateful couching-place
for beasts of the field, as well as a favorite roosting-
place for birds of evil omen. At another time,
within our memory, it was the debatable border land
of two fiercely contending religious clans, who well

nigh came from words to blows in disputing their
mutual claims to rightful possession. And, lastly,
in the height of the late terrific contest between
the States it was again converted into a barracks
for the accommodation of a choice band of self-
sacrificing heroes of the last ditch, who generously
forewent their share of the splendid laurels which
bloom on the perilous ridges of battle and beside
the paths of crimson glory, and were humbly content with the meaner sort that grew in the neighboring morass, in which they found at once the
modest recompense of a soldier's reward and a
secure hiding-place from the insolent foe. Away
with mawkish whimpering and sentimental cant!
What is yonder ancient pile of brick and mortar
but the rude work of profane human hands, and as
for those mournful relics of the forgotten dead,
why, if every grave were covered with a stone the
surface of the earth would in no while become
one vast tessellated pavement of lying epitaphs. The
moral is plainly written: You must do something
more than "building churches," if you would not
have your name buried in the tomb of oblivion by
the next unvenerating generation.

Mr. Richard Alloway prognosticated rightly; there
was a large concourse of people of both sexes and
all sizes, and of different complexions of color and
creed, to hear the word expounded by that interloping schismatic, as he was obstinately denounced
by the most bigoted churchmen. The ill-natured
sneers at the Presbyterian preacher's expense only
the more inflamed the popular heart, which was
now thoroughly imbued with the sentiment of re-

ligious toleration. The services had not begun
when our friends arrived; it yet lacked some minutes of the appointed hour, and the minister had
not made his appearance. The greater part of the
male portion of the congregation, sheltered from
the blast under the lee of the church, were ex-
changing neighborly greetings and descanting upon
current news, prominently the exciting occurrences
of the previous day. Presently there is a cautionary
whisper; the conversation ceases, and all eyes are
turned upon the tall, spare, clerical-looking gentleman who, conducted by Lucy Graeme, walks quickly
across the yard to the side entrance of the church,
receiving, as he passed, the respectful salutations
of the assembly, which he acknowledged with graceful, dignified courtesy. A murmur of approbation
betokened the favorable impression his looks and
carriage had produced, as following his example,
the crowd poured into the church until it was
filled to its utmost capacity. Never before or since
was there such another gathering within those
sacred walls. Our description is taken from a letter
in the family archives, which says that the audience were "literally jammed, crammed and packed
like herrings in a barrel,"—the writer, a bouncing
damsel of fifteen, having sat through the entire
services on her father's knee. Yet, despite the dis-
comfort, the most perfect quiet and decorum reigned,
and from beginning to end the preacher had their
undivided attention.

Mr. Waddell's sermon was appropriate to the
existing state of public affairs; his text being the
tenth verse of the seventh Psalm of David. The

19*

one great leading proposition was presented in a
compact, logical arrangement of convincing argu-
ments, and enforced by the breathed spell of genuine,
unaffected eloquence. The people of America had
invoked the help of the God of battles as their
only strength and rock of defence. On one condition only could they expect to obtain the deliver-
ance for which they prayed from Him who "judgeth
the righteous and is angry with the wicked every
day." The discourse, so unlike in matter, style
and mode of delivery to any which had ever before
emanated from that pulpit, produced a profound
and lasting impression on the vast congregation,
and good Mr. John Graeme, overjoyed to see how
much his neighbors were affected by the "halesame
screed," could not have been more happy had the
sweet bells of Saint Mungo been chiming in his
ears. It was matter of becoming pride and grat-
ulation to his dying day, that memorable visitation
of grace, as he was wont to call it. The sermon
was such as might have been expected from the
wonderful preacher then in the vigorous prime of
manhood, who, long years afterwards, grown feeble
with age, palsied, sightless, yet all, more inwardly
illumined with celestial light, extorted a glowing
tribute from one who knew himself how to touch
with a master's hand the chords of human thought,
passion and feeling. The services were concluded
by a fervent appeal to the Lord of Hosts that He
would sustain and cheer the hearts and nerve the
arms of the people in the struggle which was before
them, and speedily guide them by the path of
victory to peace and freedom. The people went

away pondering deeply on what they had heard, and even 'Squire Littleton was constrained to acknowledge that the "new-light" doctrines were in the main sound and scriptural, albeit there was no good word spoken in behalf of his persecuted saints, the blessed Stuarts.

It was observed that Mary Littleton did not come to church. Lucy explained her absence in a whisper to Dick Alloway; she had remained at Bonhill to bear Mrs. Graeme company. As the congregation were dispersing Mr. Graeme drew his young neighbor one side, and imparted to him a piece of news which astonished him to an extraordinary degree. He gave one prolonged whistle, and then suddenly remembering where he was as he met Lucy's surprised look, he blushed to the roots of his hair, clumsily fastened the carriage door on the skirt of the old gentleman's coat, and went to seek his horse in utter bewilderment and confusion.

"Wonders will never cease, Harry," he exclaimed when they were gotten clear of the crowd; "Mike Burke has disappeared; gone in the night, the Lord knows where."

"The mischief!" replied Harry, with an incredulous stare. "How did you learn that?"

"From Mr. Graeme, who had it directly from the sailor's wife," said Dick. "He stole away in his boat under the cover of darkness without a word of warning, and left no clew to his intentions save a piece of plank stuck endwise in the sand, on which he had sketched with charcoal the picture of a ship under full sail with a small boat following in her wake."

"Which means plain enough that Mike has deserted to the enemy," said Harry. "He'll have a lively time cruising after the *Katrine* in this weather. Well, it can't be helped, and really I don't see why you should be so much troubled about it in one way or the other. Your jolly old sea-dog has as much right as anybody else to choose sides in the fight; and having once served with credit in his Majesty's navy, he has only gone back to his first love. That's my solution of the matter, leaving out of view the probability of domestic provocations too grievous to be borne."

"He was well posted about the vessel's movements," Dick went on to say. "She did not put directly to sea as we supposed, but will run into the Rappahannock to complete her cargo, touching at Hobb's Hole and Merry Point; Mr. Osborn, on winding up his affairs here, having exchanged his negroes with Col. James Gordon, of Lancaster, for tobacco. The rascal could easily intercept her with a fair wind. Conrad and Archie out of their clutches, I wish they were at the bottom of the ocean."

Harry made no reply to this wrathful explosion; it was plain that Dick was in no mood for trifling. He was both deeply mortified and sorely distressed. Mike's shameful flight was the unkindest cut of all; it was the culmination of black ingratitude.

END OF PART I.

www.ingramcontent.com/pod-product-compliance
Lightning Source LLC
Chambersburg PA
CBHW020118030726
47498CB00006B/2170